THE WIZARDS' BANQUET

Other books by Vivian French

The Adventures of Alfie Onion
The Cherry Pie Princess
Tom & Tallulah and the Witches' Feast
The Dragon's Breakfast
The Giants' Tea Party
The Steam Whistle Theatre Company
The Runaways of Haddington Hall

Tales from the Five Kingdoms:
The Robe of Skulls
The Bag of Bones
The Heart of Glass
The Flight of Dragons
The Music of Zombies
The Snarling of Wolves

THE WIZARDS'
BANQUET

VIVIAN FRENCH

illustrated by **Marta Kissi**

**WALKER
BOOKS**

This is a work of fiction. Names, characters, places and incidents
are either the product of the author's imagination or, if real, are
used fictitiously. All statements, activities, stunts, descriptions,
information and material of any other kind contained herein are
included for entertainment purposes only and should not be relied
on for accuracy or replicated as they may result in injury.

First published 2022 by Walker Books Ltd
87 Vauxhall Walk, London SE11 5HJ

2 4 6 8 10 9 7 5 3 1

Text © 2022 Vivian French
Illustrations © 2022 Marta Kissi

The right of Vivian French and Marta Kissi to be identified as
author and illustrator respectively of this work has been asserted in
accordance with the Copyright, Designs and Patents Act 1988

This book has been typeset in Berkeley Oldstyle Book

Printed and bound by CPI Group (UK) Ltd, Croydon CR0 4YY

British Library Cataloguing in Publication Data:
a catalogue record for this book is available
from the British Library

ISBN 978-1-4063-9909-7

www.walker.co.uk

For Ben and Osian,

with much love

— *V.F.*

To my best friend and husband James

— *M.K.*

Chapter One

"Give you a job? Don't make me laugh!" The fishmonger bent down and took hold of Pippin's ear. "You listen to me, little sprat – run back home to your mammy, and don't come bothering folks like me when we've work to do. Do you hear me?"

"Yes!" And with a wriggle and a squirm Pippin pulled himself free, and ran off down the road. Not to his mother, however. Pippin lived with his great aunt – and she was as fierce as the fishmonger, if not more so. Years of sweeping and scrubbing other people's houses had hardened her heart as well as her hands. She had woken Pippin early that morning, and as he ate his lumpy porridge she had announced that the moment had come for him to leave home.

"Pippin Potts! I'm sick and tired of having you under my feet all day. It's high time you looked after yourself. Here's your hat, and here's your coat – and here's a bag with an apple, a cheese sandwich, and a pair of clean socks. I don't want you back here until you've found yourself a job – and I'm not at all sure I'll want to see you then. Do you understand?"

"But where am I going to find a job?" Pippin had stared in bewilderment.

"There's a town just down the road, isn't there?" His great aunt had folded her arms, and frowned. "And what do you find in a town?"

"Erm … people?"

"Shops! There'll be a butcher, a baker – all sorts. Use your wits – if you've got any, that is. One of them's sure to want a little lad like you to run errands. Be off with you!" And Pippin was shooed away as if he were a bluebottle.

Pippin had done his best to follow his great aunt's instructions. He had asked the butcher and the baker if they wanted a boy to help them, and they had said no. So had the greengrocer and the tailor, and the large woman in the hardware shop had just laughed at him. The fishmonger had been his last hope – so what was he to do now?

Inkleworth called itself a town, but it was little more than one long street with shops on either side … and Pippin had reached the far end. In front of him were fields and hills;

with the vague idea that he might find a farm, and be a farmer's boy, he walked on.

I can't go home, he thought. *Great Aunt'll be ever so angry! Besides—* he stopped for a moment to consider. *Do I want to go home?* With a skip of his heart he realized that he didn't. Home meant endless chores, and never being praised or thanked; the best he could hope for was a brief pat on the head. *I'll find something,* Pippin told himself. *Try, try and try again, that's what I'm going to do. I cleaned out the smelly old hen house, didn't I? Even if it did take ages. And if I can do that, I'm sure I can find a job!*

Remembering that he hadn't eaten since his bowl of cold porridge early that morning, he hopped over the roadside ditch, settled himself on a patch of grass, and opened the bag he'd been given. He was surprised to find a small parcel at the bottom; tearing off the wrapping paper, he found a jar containing some kind of glutinous green substance. A label stuck on the side informed

him that this was A Very Special
Turnip Pickle, and written
underneath in his great aunt's
spidery writing was the message,
A parting gift for Pippin.

"Wow! A present!" Pippin
eagerly twisted off the lid – and
gasped. The smell was so incredibly strong that his
eyes began to water, and he hurriedly put the lid
back on whilst holding his nose.

"Euch!" Making sure the jar was tightly closed,
Pippin considered it. Should he throw it away? He
was certain that he would never ever be tempted
to eat any of the contents. On the other hand, he
had never been given a present before. Deciding
he'd keep it for the time being, Pippin dropped
the jar back into his bag, and took out his picnic.
His apple was small and withered, and the cheese
sandwich was stale, but he ate hungrily.

When he had finished, he looked round to
see if there was a stream so he could quench his

thirst, but the ditch was dry and there was no stream in sight. With a sigh, he stood up. *If I can find a farm, perhaps they'll give me a drink of milk*, he thought. *Or at least a drink of water.*

He was about to set off again when a scrap of crumpled paper tied to a gatepost caught his eye.

Helpful Boy
Wanted!
Must be good
with puzzles!
Green door, top of
Grabbling Hill.

If the scratchy message hadn't been written in bright purple ink Pippin wouldn't have given it a second glance; as it was, he went to see what it said.

Helpful Boy Wanted!
Must be good with puzzles!
Green door, top of Grabbling Hill.

Pippin's heart beat faster. Helpful? He was sure he was helpful. He'd had to help all his life. He'd never been thanked, but he knew how to wash and clean and look after chickens. Good with puzzles? He didn't know. He'd never had to solve one … but he was sure that he could try. He pulled the paper off the post, and tucked it in his pocket.

There was a small hill to the left to the road; hoping that this was Grabbling Hill, Pippin climbed over the gate and set off up the narrow winding path on the other side.

Grabbling Hill was steeper than it looked; by the time Pippin arrived at the crooked little cottage tucked in between a couple of tall pine trees he was out of breath, and thirstier than ever. Much to his relief the cottage had a green door; Pippin walked towards it with his fingers crossed behind his back, and counted his steps for luck.

"Odd numbers and I get a job, even numbers and I don't," he told himself – and exactly as he reached ninety-nine the green door was flung open and a small bespectacled figure came bustling out.

"So you're here at last! Took your time, didn't you? Come along, come along! Your dinner's getting cold!"

Pippin's jaw dropped. "Ummm…" he said. "I'm Pippin… Pippin Potts. You don't know me…"

"Know you?" The owner of the cottage stared at Pippin. "What does that matter? I advertised for a boy – a helpful sort of boy – and here you are! Come in, come in!"

Pippin, his head whirling, did as he was asked. As he followed the little old man, he noticed that the faded purple coat he was wearing was covered in stars, and his hat might once have been pointed before it collapsed with age. Feeling a little anxious, he asked, "Excuse me but … you're not a wizard, are you?"

"Of course I am!" The wizard swung round and beamed at Pippin. "Didn't I introduce myself? No? Dearie, dearie me. Now, let me see… Can I remember my name? Aha! It's a good day! I'm Abacus Peridot, second level wizard, and four hundred and seventy-three years old. Or am I four hundred and thirty-seven? Never mind. It doesn't matter. How do you do?"

And he held out a withered old hand.

Chapter Two

The inside of the wizard's cottage was so extraordinary that Pippin forgot all Great Aunt Gert's rules about politeness, and stared. He had never seen such a mess: ancient books and curling sheets of paper and pens and pencils and bottles of ink were all jumbled up together.

The chairs were heaped with yet more books, and there was also a surprising amount of wool; Abacus seemed to be fond of knitting. A table in the centre of the room was groaning under the weight of variously assorted jars and bottles containing liquids of every colour of the rainbow, and half open boxes full of herbs and powders were balanced one on top of another in the most precarious way. Pippin was sure that if he so much as sneezed there'd be a landslide, so he stood very still.

Abacus waved a hand at his chaotic belongings. "I tidied up before you came. Didn't want to frighten you! And I've packed our bags. All the same, you might want to check I've thought of everything."

He began to hunt in one pocket after another. "I made a list! Where is it? Where is it? I'm sure I put it in my pocket … or did I? Maybe I dropped it somewhere?" And he dived under the table, knocking over a tottering pile of dirty cups and saucers as he did so.

Pippin watched in wonder as the wizard scrabbled about, emerging the other side of the table with a cobweb draped over his shoulders. "Not there. Never mind, it'll turn up. Or not. Don't just stand there, boy! Eat your dinner!"

Pippin, seeing no sign of any dinner anywhere, made an apologetic coughing noise. "Ermmm … thank you. But … where is it?"

"What?" Abacus Peridot peered at Pippin over the top of his glasses. "You can't find it? Oh dear. Oh dearie, dearie me. I must have shut her in by mistake."

He bounced away from the table, and pulled on a rope at the side of the room. Immediately there was a rumbling noise followed by the peal of bells … and a cupboard door flew open. A small iron cooking pot with four stout little legs came scuttling out, and positioned itself at Pippin's side. There was such a wonderful smell of stew and onions that Pippin's mouth began to water; looking down, he could see the pot was full to the brim.

"You'll need a spoon," Abacus said, and he took one from the table, wiped it on his coat, and handed it to Pippin. "There you are. Eat up. We'll be leaving later this afternoon."

Pippin was much too hungry to bother about the possible state of the spoon. He dipped it in the pot … and his first mouthful was so delicious that he nearly cried. Never, in all his life, had he tasted anything as good.

The wizard watched Pippin as he ate, and ate … then ate some more. "She's a good little pot, isn't she? Don't let me forget her, boy. We'll need her on our journey. Here – have a drink."

And Abacus picked one of the dirty cups off
the floor, and waved a hand over it. Immediately
it was sparkling clean and then, as Abacus waved
his hand a second time, Pippin saw it fill with rich
creamy milk.

"WOW," he breathed. "That's MAGIC!"

The wizard chuckled. "So it is. And very useful,
too. Haven't washed a cup or a plate for at least
a hundred years. Boring kind of occupation, I've
always thought."

"Oh, it is."

Pippin's reply was heartfelt. He had been
washer-upper-in-chief ever since he was tall
enough to reach the sink, and he had never ever
enjoyed the experience.

He drank his milk with enthusiasm, wiped his
mouth, and put the cup back down on the floor.

As he did so, a thought came to him, and he
nodded to the little iron pot.

"Thank you," he said. "That was the best meal
I've ever eaten!"

The pot jumped, twirled round twice, and skipped back into the cupboard, slamming the door behind her.

"Don't be offended." The wizard rubbed his nose. "She's hiding. She's not that fond of travelling. You might need to carry her now and then. You won't mind, will you?"

"No." Pippin hesitated. "Um … you said we were going on a journey? Where are we going?"

"I haven't the faintest idea." Abacus tapped the table for emphasis, and a glass bottle fell off and crashed to the floor, leaving a pool of green liquid that bubbled and steamed before sinking into the carpet. "That's up to you, boy. You're the one that's good at solving puzzles."

"Oh." Pippin felt a sudden wave of panic. "Um—"

"Stop saying UM." The wizard shook his finger at Pippin. "You're not a fly. You're the boy I ordered to help me, so I'm relying on you to find the way." A faint blush floated across his face. "I did have an invitation. I suppose that

 21

might have helped … but it vanished when I was tidying things. It happens, you know. I put things down, and next thing – pffft! – they're gone!"

Pippin took a moment to think how best to ask his next question. "So … when I've found the way, what exactly are you hoping to find at the other end?"

Abacus Peridot's eyes grew very wide, and he stared as if Pippin had said the stupidest thing in the whole wide world. "The Wizards' Banquet, of course! That's why I need you. The Wizards' Centenary Banquet! And I have to win." A wistful expression came over his face. "It's the most wonderful prize this year. Wonderful! A room in the Golden Bean Hotel for the rest of my life… THAT'S what I want." He closed his eyes with a blissful smile. "They've never offered a prize like that before. Just imagine it… No need to make magic. No need to do anything at all, except sit in the comfiest of chairs, and watch the rest of the world go tumbling by… Tell me, what could be better than that?"

Pippin scratched his head. "Excuse me for saying so, but aren't you comfortable here? I mean, you've got that amazing pot, and you don't need to wash any dishes, and you can magic up any drink you want…"

"No, no, no, NO." For the first time, the wizard looked serious. "Magic's a tricky beast. Takes the stuffing out of you, especially if you're only a second level wizard like me. Use it too often, and you shrink into nothingness. I'm four hundred and seventy-three – or is it thirty-seven? – years old, and I'm half the size I was. Haven't you noticed my coat? It was made two hundred years ago. Far too big for me now."

Pippin looked, and saw that Abacus was right. The coat had been tailored for a much larger figure; it was bunched up, and tied at the waist with a piece of rope. "Oh dear," he said.

Abacus nodded. "Oh dear indeed. If I shrink much more I'll be nothing more than a hat with legs. But at the Golden Bean Hotel everything'll be done for me. I won't need to lift a finger – never ever again – and I might even manage to grow a little! Now, as soon as I've shut the windows, let's get going!"

Chapter Three

As Abacus Peridot hurried away to another room, Pippin stared at the heaps of books and papers surrounding him. Might there be a map? If there was, would it tell him where to find the Golden Bean Hotel?

He took up a book at random, and there was a slither and a crash as the pile beneath slid off the table and onto the floor. As he bent to pick it up, he dislodged an enormous basket that was balanced on top of another heap of books. Multi-coloured balls of knitting wool bounced in all directions and rolled away under the table.

"Oh no!" Pippin's heart began to beat even faster. "What have I done?" Kneeling down again he began to pick up the balls and stuff them in his pockets; as he moved a battered old notebook in order to reach further under the table, an official-looking card with shining golden edges fell out from between the pages. Forgetting all about the wool Pippin pounced on it, and read,

To Master Abacus Peridot, Second Level Wizard with honours, greeting! We hereby invite you to the Wizards' Centenary Banquet, due to take place on the ninety-nineth day of this year. It will be your task to discover the place where our banquet will be held — and remember! — only one hundred wizards are invited.

Pippin took a deep breath, and stood up. One hundred wizards! Until today he hadn't known there was even one wizard in existence, let alone a hundred! Where were they all living? He looked again at the card.

Ninety-nine places will be set, and — NOTE THIS! — the ninety-ninth wizard to arrive will have no place at the table. The one hundredth wizard to arrive will win a place in the Golden Bean Hotel for the rest of his or her long and illustrious life.

"That's odd." Pippin stared at the card. "So what happens to the ninety-ninth wizard?"

As if it had heard him, the card quivered, and Pippin turned it over. In heavy black letters, there was another message.

WARNING!

The ninety-ninth wizard to arrive will IMMEDIATELY be turned into a TORTOISE.

Signed: Philostrate Bodiface, Head Wizard.

Pippin dropped the card as if it had burned him. Turned into a tortoise? What kind of arrangement was that? He had never in his entire life heard of such an extraordinary competition. How was he ever going to be able to help Abacus win?

"I'm not sure I can do this," he said out loud. "It's all so complicated."

"Easy dozey. Walky walky one step one time."

The voice was rusty and dusty, as if it wasn't used to speaking. Spinning round, Pippin saw that the cupboard door had opened, and the little iron pot was now outside. As he stared, he began to see

that she had a face, with two twinkling eyes and a wide metal smile.

Pippin blinked. So many extraordinary things had happened to him in the last half hour that he was beginning to wonder if he had fallen asleep, and was dreaming. "Erm … did you speak?" he asked.

The pot chuckled. "Can't see no peoples else than we." She came a little closer, and held out an iron leg … or could it be an arm, Pippin wondered. "How de do? Ms Latterly Pot. That's me!"

"How do you do." Pippin shook the leg, or the arm. "I … I haven't met an iron pot before. At least, not a talking one."

Latterly sniffed. "Them's not magic pots. I be special, I be."

"You certainly make the most wonderful stew," Pippin told her, and as Latterly twirled yet again he realized that this was the way she showed pleasure. He smiled at her, and as he did so Abacus appeared in a rush, and without any luggage.

"Now then!" To Pippin's astonishment, the wizard was frowning. "Who have we here? Who are you? And what are you doing in my house?"

A cold hand clutched at Pippin's stomach. He must have been dreaming … and it had all been a terrible mistake. The wizard hadn't meant to invite him in and offer him a job.

"Excuse me … I'm Pippin Potts. I found your advertisement—" he brought out the scrap of paper. "See? And you invited me in, and gave me a wonderful dinner of stew and onions."

"Never heard of such nonsense. Be off with you! Scat!" Abacus' face was blank. "Stew and onions? Ridiculous!"

"Tready tready toes!" Latterly tugged at Pippin's trouser leg. "He be done forgetting again!"

Pippin swallowed hard. It seemed both rude and ungrateful to do as the iron pot suggested, but what did he have to lose? Taking a deep breath, he trod heavily on the wizard's toes – and was rewarded by a loud shout, followed by a hand patting him on the shoulder.

"Dear boy! I do apologize!" Abacus sounded upset. "I forgot. It happens, you know… I'm so very, very sorry." He sank onto a chair. "I'm nothing more than an old has-been. How can I possibly win a place at the hotel if I can't even remember I've got a helper? Perhaps I should count my blessings, and stay here." He sighed heavily, and put his head in his hands.

"Please, Mr Abacus… Please don't give up!" Pippin's tender heart was touched by the old wizard's evident distress. "I'll help you – I promise I will. My great aunt always told me to try, try and try again, and it works – it really does. I cleaned a whole hen house once. When she ordered me to do it I was sure I couldn't – but I did it!" He hunted around on the floor until he found the invitation.

"Look! I found this! It's a sign."

Abacus sat up. "You found the invitation? Oh my goodness … what a boy you are! That'll help us! That'll help us for sure!" Jumping to his feet, he seized Pippin's hands and danced him round and round. "Oh, Pippin Potts! Let's go – let's go right now this minute!"

"But … the luggage…" Pippin was breathless.

"Who cares about the luggage? If I've got
a clever lad like you with me, we won't need
a thing! Woohoooo!" And Abacus Peridot whirled
Pippin through the door and, pausing only just
long enough for Latterly to scuttle out after them,
slammed it shut with a triumphant crash.

Once outside, the wizard looked expectantly at
Pippin. "Which way, boy?"

Pippin hesitated. He had no map, no clear
instructions, and only a name to look for. Searching
in his pockets for the invitation card, he discovered
several balls of scarlet wool; shoving them hastily
in his bag, he looked again for the card, and was
relieved to find it safely tucked away.

"Here it is," he said, and studied it, hoping
there might be a hidden clue that he had missed.

To his surprise one edge was a much brighter gold than the others; as an experiment Pippin turned the card round … and, sure enough, this time it was the other edge. He took a few tentative steps towards Inkleworth and the gold dulled; a few steps the other way, and it gleamed.

With a triumphant gesture, Pippin pointed up the road away from town. "This way!"

"Excellent!" Abacus linked his arm through Pippin's, and they set off, Latterly skipping beside them.

None of them noticed the strange little figure lurking in the dark shadows cast by the pine trees – a figure that whistled softly to itself, and drew a tick in the air with a grubby finger before creeping after them.

Chapter Four

They made slow progress. Pippin had already
walked a long way that day, and as the evening
drew on his feet felt heavier and heavier. Latterly
was struggling too; every so often she would moan,
and when Abacus announced that it was time to
stop for the night both Pippin and the iron pot
were delighted. They left the road to find shelter
under a clump of trees close by a stream, and sat
down to rest. Pippin was getting hungry again,
and he looked hopefully at Latterly – but she was
tucked up beside a tussock of grass with her eyes
firmly closed.

"I never knew cooking pots could talk," he remarked. "Have you owned her for a long time?"

"Shhh!" Abacus put his finger to his lips. "Don't let her hear you, or she'll take offence! Nobody owns a magic pot. They choose where they live. Treat them wrong, and they're off and away. Latterly's done me the honour of living with me for a couple of years, but one day that little pot will wake up, decide she needs a change – and whoops! She'll be gone. Of course, once I'm happily settled at the Golden Bean Hotel she'll be looking for a new home. Treat her right and it might even be you."

"That would be wonderful." Pippin gave Latterly another hopeful look. "Will she be cooking anything tonight, do you think?"

Abacus shrugged. "It's her decision whether she cooks or not. You'll have to wait and see. Now, excuse me but I'm going to go to sleep." And Abacus wrapped his overlarge coat tightly round him and settled down. A moment later he was snoring, and Pippin was the only one left awake. He sighed, and leant back against a tree trunk; pulling out the invitation card he studied it yet again. There was no golden glow, and in the dim light he could hardly read the letters … in fact, some seemed to have vanished altogether. Pippin rubbed his eyes and looked again. Just a few stood out; idly, Pippin put the remaining letters together.

NINE … HE … N … H … ILL…

"YES!" Pippin's shout was so loud that Abacus leapt to his feet with his fists clenched.

"Where are they? Let me at 'em! I'll stop 'em! Thunderbolts and lightning … what? What, what? What, what, what?"

"It's all right! Nobody's here." Pippin waved the invitation card in the air. "But I've just made the most amazing discovery—"

Abacus interrupted him. "Stop! Stop right there! I'm all of a dither, all of a pother. When I'm asleep, I'm asleep, and I don't like being woken up like that. Not at all. Addles the brain." He shook his head. "Not much left, you see. Not much left."

Pippin drooped. "Sorry, Master Abacus," he said. "I won't do it again."

"Good boy." And Abacus wrapped himself up in his coat again and went straight back to sleep.

"My sleepy sleepy is all gone too," said a reproachful voice, and Pippin saw that Latterly was awake.

"I'm so sorry," Pippin apologized. "It's just – I think I know where to find the party! I was looking at the invitation, you see, and I noticed—"

"Shhhh!" Latterly looked cautiously from left to right, then whispered, "There be ears! Ears that waggle waggle... Darkness brings looky

looky eyes and waggle waggle ears to catch
at words!"

"There are?" Pippin shivered. "Should I wake
up Master Abacus?"

Latterly shook herself, and Pippin realized she
meant no. He crept closer, and asked in a low
voice, "Are we in danger?"

"Is little little looker," the pot told him, "but
shiny bright eyes! Looky looky you, looky looky
me, looky looky him … and shiny shiny SHINY
when you say party!"

Pippin hastily stuffed the invitation card deep
inside his shirt. "Could it be a spy?"

Latterly rocked from side to side as if to
say maybe yes, and maybe no. When she had
righted herself she said, "Looky looker gone…
Slippy slided away."

"That's good," Pippin said, but he still
felt uncomfortable. Getting up, he tiptoed
cautiously in between the trees to check for
spies. He could see no signs of a watcher,

but as he rounded a particularly prickly gorse bush he became aware of the faint smell of peppermints. It was gone almost as soon as he noticed it, and for a moment he wondered if he could have imagined it. "But why would I imagine peppermints?" he asked himself. "No – someone was here. I'll tell Abacus in the morning." He sniffed again – and this time it wasn't peppermints that he could smell. It was hot chocolate, and it was coming from behind him.

"Oh! Oh … is that Latterly?" Pippin scrambled back as fast as he could go, and found he was right. Latterly was bubbling happily, and as Pippin appeared she called to him. "Beddy byes drink! Make you sleepy sleepy all night long."

She was right. The hot chocolate was thick and sweet and filling, and when Pippin curled himself up on a pile of leaves he felt fuller and happier than he had done for many years.

"This is a real adventure," he told himself sleepily, and then his eyes closed, and he too began to snore.

Chapter Five

"Peppermints! How many times have you been told, Kitty Scarper? NO PEPPERMINTS!" Master Boldways Grime was sitting on a small rock outcrop half a mile or so from where Pippin slept, and he was glaring at his assistant.

Half elf, half girl, Kitty Scarper was trying her best to look innocent.

Boldways coughed, and wiped his nose on a large spotted handkerchief. "It's a disgusting habit, and I won't have it, I tell you. Have you got them in your pockets? Or are they in your collecting bag?"

Kitty tried a cheery smile. "Nothing in my pockets."

"Then they're in your collecting bag." Boldways' face darkened. "Turn it out right now this minute!"

Knowing that there was an almost full paper bag of peppermints tucked in the bottom of her bag, Kitty hastily turned the conversation.

"I found out something important, Master! Ever so important!"

"You're trying to change the subject," Boldways growled. "I want to see those peppermints!"

Kitty put her head on one side.

"But Master! Don't you want to find the Wizards' Banquet?"

"What?" The peppermints were forgotten as Boldways stared at her. "Of course I do! Isn't that why I hired you?" He jumped up, and strode angrily round the rock. "That beetle-brained Head Wizard! Leaving me off the list – ME! Boldways Grime!"

Boldways, his eyes bulging and his face purple, stamped his foot so hard that three rabbits leapt out of their burrows and fled for safety.

"And writing to me in that mealy mouthed way… 'I'm sure you'll understand, Master Grime, that our places are limited to those second level wizards who would at least *try* to restrict themselves to positive and constructive acts of magic.'"

With a sneer and a twitch of his thick black eyebrows, the wizard flung himself back down.

"So yes, Kitty Scarper. I want to find the banquet. I want to find the banquet, because I want to win the prize! A room in the Golden Bean Hotel, that's what I want." Boldways' eyes gleamed. "And when I've won it, Kitty Scarper, I'll sell it. Sell it to the highest bidder … and believe you me, that'll get a lot of creaky old wizards counting their gold pieces. A hundred pieces of gold. Two hundred. Maybe –" he rubbed his hands together – "maybe even three hundred! Four! Five! And that'll show that hoity-toity Head Wizard just how constructive a second level wizard can be!"

Kitty nodded. "And I've got news. I know the way to the banquet!"

"WHAT?" Boldways sat bolt upright, his mean little eyes gleaming. "You'd better be telling the truth! Or I'll turn you into a toadstool!"

Ignoring the threat, Kitty gave her master a triumphant smile. "I watched that whiskery old wizard's house, just like you told me – and a boy came knocking at the door. Next thing, out they rush … and Master! The boy's got an invitation! It's showing him the road to travel … and where to go!"

"Hmmmm…" Boldways considered.

A calculating look came over his face, and he said, "It seems to me that we should befriend these fellow travellers. We'll be a merry party! Off we'll go together, over hill and dale. We'll let them lead us all the way to the Wizards' Banquet – and then! Guess what?"

"You'll make sure you win the prize!" Kitty said.

"Exactly! Abacus Peridot is nothing more than a doddering old numbskull." Boldways gave an unpleasant chuckle. "And there's something else. The ninety-ninth wizard is going to be changed into a tortoise, and we need to avoid that. Just suppose it was Abacus Peridot! What fun that would be... I doubt he'd ever know the difference!"

And Boldways Grime rubbed his hands together in glee, and laughed at his own joke until he was red in the face and coughing.

Kitty Scarper grinned. This was her first ever job, and she was still getting used to it. She had applied to various agencies, but had been turned down by the Fairy Godmothers' Guild when her Goodness Potential had come out at only fifty per cent. She had then tried the Hobgoblins, but they too had refused her; they required a Badness Potential of at least seventy per cent.

She was aware that Boldways was a doubtful character, but he had offered her "a position with many rewards if the outcome is successful", and it had been too tempting to refuse.

After all, she had told herself, *it's much easier to be bad than good.*

"What's the boy like?" Boldways cut into her thoughts, and Kitty shrugged.

"Just a boy. Nothing special."

Boldways' eyes grew cunning.

"Make friends with him. Start tomorrow. Get him to trust you and persuade him that two heads are better than one. Find out what he knows, and when I judge the time is right I'll bump into Abacus and then— 'Oh goodness me!' I'll say. 'Fancy us both being invited! Why don't we journey together? SUCH an excellent idea!'"

"Whatever you say, Master." Kitty bowed.

"So that's settled." Boldways gave a decisive nod. "Now, find yourself somewhere to sleep, and don't snore. I can't abide snoring."

And with that, he wrapped himself up in his cloak and settled down in a grassy dip behind the rock he'd been sitting on. Two minutes later he was snoring so loudly that Kitty was forced to cover her ears as she walked away to look for somewhere to sleep herself.

Chapter Six

Pippin Potts woke with a jump. There was a mouth-watering smell of frying bacon… Staring round, he saw Abacus asleep under his wizard's coat, his whiskers trembling at each breath.

"Hungry?" Latterly came scuttling towards him.

Pippin nodded, and the iron pot grinned at him. "Bacon sandwiches," she said, and Pippin's eyes lit up.

"How ever did you do that?" he asked.

"No do questions, no get lies," Latterly told him, and she winked as Pippin helped himself to an enormous sandwich. As he sat back to enjoy it, Abacus stirred, yawned, and stretched.

"Latterly looking after you, is she?" he asked, and Pippin, his mouth too full to speak, gave him a thumbs up.

Abacus yawned again. "Good, good. Delighted to hear it." A puzzled expression floated over his face. "Remind me of your name again, young man."

"Pippin," Pippin told him. He was beginning to get used to the wizard's erratic memory. "And we're on our way to the Wizards' Banquet, Master."

"We are?" Abacus stroked his beard thoughtfully. "And I want to win the prize… A room in the Golden Bean Hotel for ever and ever. I'm right, aren't I?"

"Exactly right, Master," Pippin said. "And the invitation says we should head for the Nine Hen Hills. I'm hoping we'll find another clue when we get there."

The wizard screwed up his eyes as if he was thinking very hard. "Invitation… Invitation… Don't tell me … I'm sure I can do this. YES!"

His face cleared, and he beamed at Pippin. "I've remembered! The invitation was for me! It invited me to the banquet!"

He jumped to his feet, and shook Pippin's hand so hard that Pippin winced.

"What a wonderful boy you are! Let's go. Let's go and find these Nine Hen Hills right now this minute!"

"Perhaps you should have some breakfast first?" Pippin suggested.

"No time! No time to waste!" Abacus was buttoning up his coat. "Which way, boy? Which way?"

"I think…" Pippin had pulled the invitation out of his pocket and was looking at it hopefully. "I think—" the card twitched in his hand. "Yes! This way!" And he pointed towards the distant horizon.

At once Abacus was off, striding down to the road as fast as he could go. Latterly scuttled after him, and Pippin followed. He was wondering if he would be expected to run all the way to their destination, but it wasn't long until the wizard slowed to a slightly more reasonable pace, and both Pippin and Latterly heaved a sigh of relief.

"Master Abacus…" Pippin called after him, still trying to catch his master up. "Master Abacus … there was someone watching us last night. Latterly saw them. She says whoever it was they were very little, and they seemed very interested when I mentioned the wizards' party—"

Abacus stopped dead, and stared at Pippin. "A spy?"

Latterly gave a loud squeak. "Was looky looky looking very much."

"Rattling rabbits and dancing dandelions! Why in the name of whiskers didn't you wake me up?" Abacus demanded.

"Erm…" Pippin was unable to think of a polite way to explain that he had been told not to wake his master, but Latterly had no such inhibitions.

"You say no wakey waking. Boy did as told."

"Oh yes." Abacus looked a little ashamed of himself. "So I did." He stroked his beard. "Well next time, wake me. You didn't see anything?"

Pippin shook his head. "No, but I did smell peppermints."

"Peppermints?" Abacus began to laugh. "Well, well, well … and this so-called spy was very small? It was an inquisitive child. No need to worry, boy. No need at all." And he set off again, chuckling to himself at Pippin's foolishness.

Kitty Scarper, hidden behind a blackberry bush, gave herself a mental round of applause. *Looks like peppermints can be useful after all,* she thought. *So much for Master Boldways!*

As Abacus, Pippin and Latterly continued down the road, Kitty kept as close to them as was possible. Despite her master's instructions, she had ideas of her own. *I need to practise being bad,* she told herself, *so I'm going to steal that invitation.* Pleased with her decision, she kicked hard at a pebble … and it shot ahead of her and rattled against an old tin lying at the side of the road.

"What's that?" Pippin swung round, and Kitty was forced to fling herself into a bed of nettles to avoid being seen. "Someone threw a stone!"

Abacus peered down the road. "I can't see anyone. Are you sure you didn't kick it?"

"Quite sure, Master." Pippin took a few steps back the way they had come, looking to right and left as he did so. Kitty, trying hard to ignore the painful nettle stings on her legs and arms, held her breath as he came closer. "Someone – or something – must be following us!"

"Why would they do that?" Abacus scratched his head. "You're imagining things, boy. No time to waste. No time to waste!" And the wizard set off again.

"Pippy Pip!" Latterly was circling Pippin. "My little leggy legs is tired. Picky uppy? Please, Pippy Pip?"

Glancing up the road one last time, Pippin picked Latterly up by her handle. She was heavy, but he grinned at her as she settled in the crook of his arm. "That better?"

"Betterly better best," the little pot said gratefully. "Now sleepy sleepy sleep." And she closed her eyes.

As Pippin and Abacus walked away Kitty climbed out of her bed of nettles, muttering to herself. She had decided to blame Pippin for her many stings; it was easier than admitting she had made a mistake in kicking the pebble too hard.

"The sooner I can get hold of that invitation the better. I don't see why we need him, or that ancient old wizard," she told herself as she rubbed at her arms. "If the invitation shows me and Master Boldways which way to go, we can leave them to meander about as much as they like."

Chapter Seven

Far, far away, in the Centre for Wizarding Studies, Philostrate Bodiface, the Head Wizard, was presiding over a meeting of the Centenary Banquet committee.

Tall, and so thin he hardly had a shadow, he was dressed in black velvet from head to foot; the only note of colour was the scarlet ribbon that attached a disgruntled-looking bat to his shoulder. The two wizards on either side of him were sunk deep in their chairs: one was yawning, and the other was asleep.

"Can you confirm that the invitations have been delivered, Gloaming?" Philostrate Bodiface turned to the bewhiskered wizard sitting on his right. "All one hundred of them?"

Gloaming stirred himself sufficiently to call to the goblin, standing across the room.

"Bulge! That was your job. Were the invitations delivered?"

The goblin nodded. "Yusss."

"And the invitation cards were checked before they were sent?" Philostrate went on. "They contained sufficient information to help each wizard on his journey, with plenty of obstacles to overcome?"

Gloaming peered over his glasses at the overlarge wizard opposite him. "Handily! That was your contribution, I believe?"

Handily opened one eye. "What, what, what? What kind of contribution? Old clothes? Cardboard boxes? Second-hand spells? Who's asking?"

"The invitation cards," Gloaming snapped. "You were supposed to check them."

"Oh … those things. Yes, yes, yes…" Handily's voice faded away, and his breathing became slow and steady.

"Excellent!" The Head Wizard gave a dismissive wave. "So. They'll be coming here to the Centre for Wizarding Studies from all over the country – at least, they will if they've read their cards correctly." He gave a loud and self-satisfied bark of laughter. "Our centre! The last place they'll ever think of. My dear fellow wizards, allow me to refresh your memory."

He rose to his feet, beaming at his committee of two, and Gloaming slumped in his chair. The Head Wizard was much too fond of the sound of his own voice.

Philostrate cleared his throat. "Traditionally, the venue for the Centenary Banquet has always been hidden far from here. You may remember that three hundred years ago it was held in the Druid's Circle, and two hundred years ago in the Neverending Wood. The last Centenary Banquet was in the Echoing Caves—"

"And that was a mistake." Handily had woken up again. "Couldn't hear a word anyone said. Echo,

echo, echo… Made my head hurt. A foolish notion. Very foolish."

Philostrate looked annoyed. The Echoing Caves had been his idea. "It wasn't the venue that was wrong," he said stiffly. "It was the fact that so many wizards are hard of hearing."

"Hmph!" Handily grunted. "It was a mistake!"

Handily's interruption had stopped the Head Wizard's flow, and he was now pacing up and down while studying his list.

"The important thing, gentlemen, is that the incoming wizards must be carefully checked as they arrive. There must be no mistakes – I repeat, no mistakes. The one hundredth wizard will win a room in the Golden Bean Hotel, whereas the ninety-ninth – as decided by me at our last meeting – will be turned into a tortoise by means of a Tortoise-o-meter."

He smiled a self-congratulatory smile.

"An inspired addition to the competition, even if I do say so myself."

Gloaming was doubtful. "A question, HW. If the ninety-ninth is going to be turned into a tortoise, and the hundredth is to win the prize, won't they all try to be last? Lurk in corners, hide under bushes – all that kind of thing?"

"Really, Gloaming!" Philostrate rolled his eyes. "Do you think I haven't already considered that possibility? Of course, the younger ones aren't bothered about a room in the Golden Bean Hotel. They're here for the banquet, and to gossip with each other. It's the ancient ones we need to watch. I shall cause a thick fog to surround the walls of the centre. No wizard will be able to see any of their fellows until they've passed under the arch, through the gate, and into the courtyard. In fact…" A thoughtful expression crossed his face. "I might set the fog right now, just to be on the safe side."

Gloaming was still looking doubtful. "But if there's thick fog all round the centre, how will the wizards find the entrance gate?"

The Head Wizard waved a casual hand in the air. "A little challenge. Easily solved, I have no doubt. Think of it as a test of your rather inadequate abilities, Gloaming – think of it as a test! Ha, ha, ha!" Laughing uproariously at his joke, he smoothed back his hair and inadvertently knocked the bat off his shoulder.

"Oi! Watch what you're doing!" Hissing angrily, the bat fluttered back.

Philostrate, still laughing, flicked at her and knocked her off again.

With a furious squeak, she bit the wizard's finger.

"Ouch! That HURT!" The Head Wizard scowled. "Here!" He pulled off the scarlet collar, and pushed the bat into the goblin's arms. "Throw this ungrateful beast out! Then go and find something useful to do. My fellow wizards and I need to discuss the menu for the banquet, and that's no concern of yours."

At once Gloaming and Handily sat up straight, and as the goblin marched away their voices rose in excitement as they began to list the many different dishes to be provided.

Chapter Eight

It was late that evening before Kitty Scarper saw her chance to steal the invitation. Abacus, Pippin and Latterly had chosen a grassy hollow sheltered by an old oak tree for their night's rest; Latterly had produced a tasty hotpot for supper, and the wizard and Pippin had eaten well.

Splendidly full, they were both already half asleep. It had been a long walk, but the Nine Hen Hills were now clearly in sight, and Pippin was certain that they'd be able to reach them the next day.

Pleased with their progress, Abacus covered himself with his coat and yawned.

"Well done, boy. Tell me again… What's your name?"

Pippin grinned. "Pippin, Master Abacus. And Master Abacus … can I ask you something?"

Abacus nodded. "Of course, dear boy. Ask away."

"Well… I've been thinking. You're a wizard … so couldn't you just make a spell and magic us to the Wizards' Banquet?"

His master sat bolt upright. "But boy! There'd be no competition if we wizards magicked our way there! Besides –" he pulled at his beard –"that would need a remarkable number of heavy spells, and it's like I told you. Magic takes it out of you if you're a second level wizard like me. I'd end up the size of a mouse. No, no. We have to find the way … and you're just the chap to lead us there. Where do we go tomorrow?"

Pippin was flattered by the wizard's trust in him, but disappointed that there was no way to shorten the journey. "Tomorrow we go to the Nine Hen Hills, Master."

Abacus raised an eyebrow. "NINE? Do we have to climb them all?"

"I don't know." Pippin pulled the invitation out of his pocket, and squinted at it in the fading light. Just as before, certain letters seemed to stand out, and he tried to make sense of them.

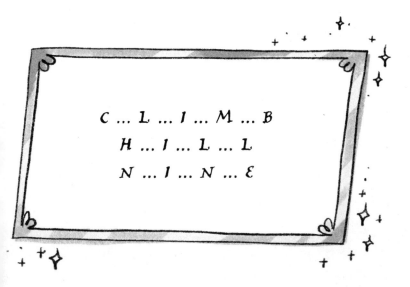

C ... L ... I ... M ... B
H ... I ... L ... L
N ... I ... N ... E

"It's telling us!" Pippin's voice rose. "It says, 'climb hill nine'!"

"I'm delighted to hear it." The wizard sounded relieved. "My poor old legs are aching. Nine hills would be eight too many…" His voice drifted into a snore, and he was asleep.

Pippin studied the card a little longer, but there was no further information to be read, and he tucked it back into his pocket. Then, with a smile at Latterly, who was dozing close beside him, he too closed his eyes.

Hidden out of sight in the branches of a nearby tree, Kitty grinned. "So! They're on

their way to the Nine Hen Hills, are they?

I wonder how they'll manage without a magic invitation to show them the way!" And she slid silently down the tree trunk.

It was the work of seconds to tiptoe over. Kitty knew exactly where to look, and Pippin didn't stir as she eased the invitation out of his pocket.

"Got it!" she breathed, and began to hurry away. Glowing with success, she didn't look where she was going and her foot brushed against the little iron pot – and Latterly opened one sleepy eye.

"Pippy pip?" she murmured. "Be that you?"

Kitty was gone before the iron pot could catch more than a glimpse of her flying figure –but it was enough.

"PIPPY PIP!" she said urgently. "Little little looker was here! Wakey wake! Wakey wake NOW!"

"What? What is it?" Pippin sat bolt upright, his hair on end. "What's happening?"

"Little little looker," Latterly repeated. "Was here! Was looky looking… I seed it!"

Pippin stared wildly round. "I can't see anyone… Are you sure?"

"Sure as eggsies is eggsies."

"But what could they be looking for? We haven't got anything!" But a sudden terrible thought came to Pippin, and he dug in his pockets.

"Oh nooooo…" His mouth went dry, and his heart began to pound in his chest. Frantically he checked every pocket again and again – but it was true. The invitation had vanished.

Leaping to his feet Pippin rushed first one way and then the other, but the night had swallowed the intruder.

With a groan he flung himself back on the ground. "What am I going to say to Master Abacus? I've failed him! Why didn't I look after it better?"

Latterly made a soothing noise. "Sleepy sleep now, Pippy Pip. All better when the sunny sun shines."

But Pippin could not be soothed. He tossed and he turned while his mind whirled. What would Abacus do when he discovered the loss of the magic invitation? He was sure to be angry. Would he send him home in disgust?

I can't go home… I just can't! Pippin told himself. *I'll tell Master Abacus I'll hunt the thief down, whatever it takes. He trusted me – and I really, really want to help him win his prize! He's been so kind to me… Oh why, oh why, did this have to happen?*

A tear trickled down his cheek, and Pippin didn't try to wipe it away. He pulled his tunic over his head and cried until he finally drifted into an uneasy sleep.

*   *   *

Boldways Grime was dreaming a very satisfactory dream. He had somehow cheated an extraordinary amount of gold out of a frail old lady, and he was happily tying it up in sacks when he was woken by Kitty Scarper shaking him hard.

"Master! Master! I've got the invitation! Look – it's here! So we don't need that silly old wizard and his boy – we can find the banquet without them!"

"What, what, what? Invitation? Where?" Boldways was not pleased to be shaken awake.

Kitty handed it to him, and he turned the card round and round … but nothing happened. It stayed blank, and he scowled at Kitty.

"It doesn't work! What have you done, you stupid elf? I told you to make friends with the boy! Get him to lead us, to show us the way."

Kitty stared at him, shocked by his response. "But Master—" she began, only to be cut short by the furious Boldways.

"Take the invitation back! Take it back AT ONCE, I say! And if you dare to disobey me again, I'll turn you into a slippery slimy slug and stamp on you."

"Yes Master – I mean, no Master. I'm on my way, Master! I'm on my way!" Kitty, pale and shaking, ran.

As soon as she was out of sight, she slowed down. There had been such an unpleasant look in Boldways' eyes that she was, for the first time in her life, genuinely scared. For a moment she wondered if she should throw away the invitation card and have another attempt at joining the Fairy Godmothers' Guild, but her pride prevented her.

That would be giving in, she told herself, *and Kitty Scarper doesn't ever give in.* She walked a little further, still thinking. *I'll do as he says for now, but I'll keep my eyes and ears open. Master Boldways said I'd get rewarded if he won, but if he doesn't – well, I'll have to think again. There'll be a hundred wizards rumbling about at this banquet... Surely I can find* one *who could use a helpful assistant like me!*

And with this thought, she set off at a steady trot towards the field where Pippin, Latterly and Abacus were spending the night.

Chapter Nine

Pippin woke with a sick feeling at the pit of his stomach. He blinked, and rubbed at his eyes while he tried to think what was wrong – and then it hit him. The invitation! It had been stolen, and now he had to confess to Abacus. He sat up with a groan – and saw a strange girl sitting opposite him. Or *was* she a girl? Her ears were very pointed … and her eyes very green.

But I'm travelling with a wizard and a magic iron pot, Pippin told himself. *Maybe I've met an elf?* And he tried not to stare.

"Hello," Kitty said. "I found something that I think might be yours." She waved the invitation card under Pippin's nose. "It was… It was blowing down the road."

Pippin was so relieved to see the invitation that he didn't think to ask any questions.

"Thank you very, very much!" His eyes shone. "I thought it had been stolen! It was in my pocket when I went to sleep last night, but then Latterly woke me up because she heard something – and it was gone!"

Kitty shrugged. "Maybe you were sleepwalking. Who's Latterly?"

"Oh – this is!" Pippin pointed to the little iron pot, then frowned. There was no cheerful smile: Latterly looked for all the world like an ordinary cooking pot … certainly not a magic one.

"If you say so." Kitty was thinking hard. Should she say that she had already seen the pot skipping along the road? And heard her talking to Pippin? Deciding this was too risky, she gave Pippin a conspiratorial wink as she glanced at the sleeping Abacus. His eyes were closed but his mouth was wide open, and every so often an ear-splitting snore shook the grassy hollow. "Travelling with a wizard, are you? Me too."

"You're travelling with a wizard?" Pippin looked at her in astonishment. "Are you going to the Wizards' Banquet?"

As soon as he had spoken he wondered if he had said too much, but Kitty nodded, and put her finger to her lips. "Shh! You know that, and

I know that, but we don't want anyone else to know, do we?"

"No." Pippin was reassured. "What's your wizard's name?"

"Boldways Grime," Kitty said, and she got to her feet. "I'd probably better go back to him." She paused, considering. So far everything was going well: the boy hadn't asked any awkward questions, and he seemed ridiculously pleased to talk to her.

For a moment she thought how nice it would be to have him as a friend, but she squashed the idea. She was fifty per cent bad, and she had a job to do.

Kitty took a couple of steps as if she was leaving, then stopped.

"Oh! I've had an idea! Maybe we could travel together? Do you think your master would like that?" For a moment, she allowed herself to be genuine. "I would."

Pippin tried not to look astonished. In his experience, people didn't tend to want to be friends with him.

"I'll ask Master Abacus as soon as he wakes up," he said. "I'm sure he'll be pleased – he's very kind, although he's a bit forgetful sometimes."

"Tell you what," Kitty said. "I'll go and have a chat with my master, and if he thinks it's a good idea we'll meet you somewhere on the road. Where are you heading today? We're going to the Nine Hen Hills. We're going to climb to the top of—" Which hill was it that Pippin had mentioned? She took a guess. "Hill Nine."

Pippin clapped his hands. "We're going there too!"

"Then we're bound to meet again," Kitty said. "Oh – I should have asked before. What's your name? I'm Kitty Scarper."

"I'm Pippin Potts," Pippin said. "See you soon, Kitty Scarper!"

"That you will," Kitty told him … and then she was gone.

As soon as Kitty was out of sight, Latterly opened her eyes.

"Her was little looky looker," she said. "Be very careful, Pippy Pip! Her didn't find invitation. Her stole it, creepy creep in the night!"

Pippin blinked. "But if she stole it, why did she give it back to me?"

Latterly gave her version of a shrug. "Her be up to something."

Pippin was about to say that he liked Kitty, but he was interrupted by Abacus waking up with a jump.

"What, what, what? Where am I?"

He peered first at Pippin, then at Latterly.

"Boy? Latterly? What are we doing here? Why aren't we at home?"

Yet again, Pippin patiently explained that they were on their way to win the competition, and the wizard gradually calmed down. "Oh yes, yes, yes. Of course."

He smoothed his beard, and smiled at Pippin.

"We're on our way to the Chicken Hills… I remember now."

"That's right." Pippin smiled back. "And Master… There was a girl here earlier – at least, I think she was a girl. She had very pointed ears." Pippin paused while he thought about Kitty. "She moved very quietly … almost like a fairy."

"Pointed ears? That sounds like an elf." Abacus raised his eyebrows. "What did she want?"

Pippin took a deep breath. Despite Latterly's warning, he was still hoping to see Kitty again. "She's working for another wizard who's going to the banquet, and she wondered if we could all travel together."

Abacus was interested. "Another wizard? What's his name?"

"Boldways Grime," Pippin said.

Abacus shook his head. "Never heard of him. Not that that means anything, mind. We wizards don't mix much. Of course, he could be an imposter."

"Kitty said they were heading for the Nine Hen Hills," Pippin said. "Surely they wouldn't have known that was the right way unless he was a real wizard?"

"An excellent point, dear boy." Abacus nodded. "Well … if we happen to bump into them, we can have a little chat and see how we get along together. But I'm hungry!" He looked hopefully at Latterly. "Might there be anything on offer?"

But the little iron pot didn't answer. Pippin had offended her by his defence of Kitty Scarper, and he and Abacus had to set out on the road with their stomachs rumbling. As they walked Pippin kept one hand on the invitation in his pocket, just in case he lost it again … and, gradually, he began to wonder if Latterly could be right about Kitty.

He rubbed his head, and tried to puzzle it out. He could understand her stealing his magic invitation if she was working for another wizard – after all, Abacus had managed to lose his – but why had she brought it back? With a sigh, Pippin gave up, and decided that if he and Kitty met up again he would be more careful. He looked down at Latterly, who was stomping along beside him with a fierce expression on her face.

"I've been thinking," he said apologetically, "and you could be right. There was something strange about Kitty."

The iron pot gave him a sideways look. "Good, Pippy Pip." She gave a little hop. "Now we be friendy friends again." She hopped again … and the comforting smell of chicken and potatoes floated into the air, making Pippin's mouth water and Abacus come to a sudden halt.

"Breakfast?" he asked. "Or is it lunch?"

Pippin was already peering in the pot. "Chicken stew," he said.

Abacus flung himself down at the side of the road. "Excellent!" He pulled two spoons out of his pocket and handed one to Pippin. "Here, lad… What's your name again?"

"Pippin," Pippin said happily, and he and Abacus settled down to eat.

Chapter Ten

As the goblin stomped along the corridor towards the back door and the courtyard beyond, the bat fluttered in his hands.

"Euch," she said. "Wizard's blood! Does you no good, that stuff. Got a shocking stomach ache."

The goblin didn't answer. He was unbolting the heavy back door to the wizards' centre; once it was open he waited for the bat to fly away, but she stayed perched on his wrist.

"Oh my," she complained. "My poor stomach. Don't suppose you've got an indigestion pill somewhere about you?" Seeing the goblin's blank expression, she went on, "No. I thought as much. I'll just have to hope I don't turn into a caterpillar on the way home. Wizard's blood – I should have known better. Ma warned me when I took the job. 'Don't you go biting any of them there wizards, Mavis,' she told me. 'Magic blood, that's what they've got! Never know what it'll do to you!' Still … that'll teach him to push me around. Should have bitten him yonks ago. Never been so bored in all my life. Like working for him, do you?"

"Yusss," the goblin said, but he didn't sound convincing, and Mavis winked at him.

"Guess you have to say that. Never know who might be listening, do you? Ooooooooh…"

She wrapped her wings round her small furry body, and rocked to and fro.

"Owwww! My stomach really, really hurts! You don't mind if I wait here for a moment longer, do you? If I'm going to turn into a caterpillar I'd rather not do it halfway home."

The goblin's reply was to sit down on the doorstep, and Mavis made herself more comfortable.

"Quiet kind of chap, aren't you? Now, I like a bit of a chat, I do – although I've not had much of a chance since I been working here. That High Wizard – he never stops talking, and he's not interested in answers. Stuck on his shoulder, all I heard was blah blah blah! All day, every day. Take this here competition what they were on about this morning. Prizes, winners, losers – there's nothing what I don't know. Be glad to be shot of it, and that's a fact."

"Yusss." The goblin agreed. "Yusss, yusss, yusss."

"Well…" Mavis struggled to her feet. "I suppose I'd better be on my way, stomach ache or no stomach ache." She stretched her wings, and winced. "Don't suppose I could trouble you for a bit of a send-off? Big strong lad like you – I'd be ever so grateful."

Rubbing his large green nose, the goblin nodded. Standing up, he pointed towards the distant horizon, but Mavis shook her head.

"Other direction, if you please. The Neverending Wood, that's where I'm headed."

"Euch." The goblin stopped, and peered at the bat. "Spots," he said. "Yun, doo, tree … lots spots."

"What?" The bat looked sideways.

The goblin was right. Small green spots were popping up on her wings and on her feet.

"OOOOOOOOH," she wailed, and then, "I got to get home! I got to get home NOW!"

"Yusss." The goblin flexed his muscles and tossed Mavis towards the clouds.

"Wheeeeee!" Up and up she flew, then zigzagged away until she could no longer be seen.

Grunting, the goblin stomped back into the wizards' centre. As he did so, a coil of thick white fog oozed out of the door.

It twisted its way across the courtyard, and under the arch that led to the outer world … and slowly but surely, the fog wrapped the Centre for Wizarding Studies in a concealing blanket.

Chapter Eleven

The rest of the walk to the Nine Hen Hills was peaceful. Abacus and Pippin had no idea that Kitty was keeping them in view, and Latterly, if she had any suspicions, kept them to herself.

Boldways had taken a different route; he was intending to meet Abacus on the top of Hill Nine, and greet him with every possible expression of surprise and delight. His plan involved a steep climb, and he was puffing by the time he reached the top. His timing was perfect; as he emerged from a clump of trees he could see Abacus, Pippin and Latterly toiling up the regular path.

He waved merrily, and called out, "Good day, fellow travellers!" As he spoke Kitty slipped from behind a large bramble bush, and came to stand beside him.

"Look, Master!" Pippin, despite his resolutions, was delighted to see Kitty again. "There's the girl I told you about. And that must be the wizard she's working for…"

Abacus squinted at Boldways. "Hmmm. Don't recognize him." He gave a half wave back. "Good day to you too, sir."

Boldways smiled an oily smile as Abacus reached the summit. "I rather think, dear sir, that we are on a similar mission. Does the word, 'banquet' have any particular significance for you?"

"It does indeed." Abacus gave Boldways a conspiratorial wink. "And would the words, 'Golden Bean' mean anything to you?"

Boldways' smile grew wider. "Absolutely." He winked back. "And would it be fair to suggest that we must both beware of the number ninety-nine?"

"Shake my hand, sir!" Abacus beamed at his fellow wizard. "A pleasure to meet you."

As the two shook hands, Pippin looked at Kitty, expecting her to be pleased, but she was staring at the ground. She was in a muddle; half of her wanted to smile at him – but she was working for Boldways, and Boldways and Abacus were rivals.

Abacus was glowing with excitement. "Let us travel together, dear sir!" He dropped his voice to a whisper. "My assistant – whose name temporarily escapes me – has the means to find the way. Boy! Come here, and show my esteemed colleague the invitation!"

He turned to Boldways, then stopped, and clutched his head. "How foolish I am! Of course –

you'll have an invitation of your own! How else would you have got this far? Forgive me, sir. It's age. That's what it is. Age. Boy – put the card away."

"Ho, ho, ho!" Boldways gave what he hoped was a hearty laugh. He knew he was on dangerous ground; his mind was whirling as he tried to decide how to explain that he had no invitation. An idea came to him. "Indeed I did. But unlike your boy, Master Abacus, my servant is a useless bag of bones." He shook his head wearily to give himself time to work out the rest of his story. "Would you believe that she dropped the precious invitation while we were crossing a river? The invitation was swept away … off it floated … never to be seen again."

"No problem, my friend," Abacus said cheerfully. "If it hadn't been for my boy here, I too would have lost my invitation." He paused, and pulled at his bushy beard. "I fear it escapes me exactly how … but no matter. No matter! Let us travel together! Boy – which way?"

Pippin pulled out the card a second time, and peered at it. To his astonishment it was blank.

"Well?" Boldways was impatient, but Abacus made a soothing noise.

"Give the boy time, dear sir. Magic mustn't be hurried, as you know."

Wondering what had gone wrong, Pippin moved a little way away from the two wizards … and letters began to appear. He took a step back, and the letters faded.

"Come along, come along!" Boldways snapped, and Pippin jumped. The wizard was all smiles when he spoke to Abacus, but his eyes were cold and calculating when he looked at Pippin.

"If you please, sir – I think I need to take it further away," he said.

Abacus nodded wisely. "Try down the hill, boy."

Grateful for the excuse to move away from Boldways, Pippin did as he was told. As soon as he was hidden from view, letters came flickering up.

Cross the Rumbling Rocks, then on to the Neverending Wood. Once there—

The letters vanished, and Pippin looked up to see Kitty was standing beside him. Her expression was unreadable as she said, "I need to tell you. I can't be friends with you. Not proper friends."

Pippin blinked. "But you said you wanted us to travel together…"

Kitty took a deep breath. "I was ordered to say that by Master Boldways." And with that she turned and ran up the hill.

Pippin sighed, and scrambled back to where the wizards were waiting. "We've got to cross the Rumbling Rocks," he announced, "and then go on to the Neverending Wood."

"Well done!" Abacus gave Pippin a pat on the back. "Which way do we go?"

Kitty was ahead of them. "The rocks are over there," she said. "Look!"

The two wizards and Pippin followed the direction of her pointing finger, and saw she was right. A winding path led down the hill, across an expanse of rough open ground, and eventually to a ravine as wide as a mighty river. Instead of rushing water, however, it was filled with enormous rocks, rocks that were heaving up and down. Concentrating, he could hear the sound of the massive boulders crashing together, and he swallowed. How could they possibly get across without getting hurt?

Kitty was watching him. "I'll make a bet with you," she said. "If I get across first, you give me that invitation! And if you get over first, I … I'll be nice to you." And she was gone, before Pippin could answer.

Chapter Twelve

As the party set off, Kitty kept away from Pippin.

"She'll never be nice to me, Latterly," he grumbled, kicking at a stone. "She even *told* me she couldn't be my friend."

"Never mind, Pippy Pip." Latterly was by his feet. "You is my bestie friendy friend." She gave him a hopeful look. "Carry? My tippy tippy toes is sore."

Pippin bent down and picked her up. "You were right about Kitty." He sighed. "I thought I'd enjoy adventuring, but it seems like ever such hard work."

Latterly gave a little chuckle. "Slow and careful does win the game, Pippy Pip."

"If you say so." Pippin refused to be comforted. "But listen! Those rocks are walloping into each other! We'll be squished and squashed for sure."

"Squishy squishy squashy squashy!" Latterly giggled. "But Pippy Pip! You can do it! Rocks is nothing. Wait and see!"

It was nearly evening before the travellers finally reached the ravine and Pippin stared in amazement. The boulders were sweeping from one side to the other like enormous waves – but unlike waves, they were solid rock.

"Well I never!" Boldways scowled at Pippin. "You've made a mistake, Pippin Potts. There's no way we can get across here."

Pippin looked at Abacus for help, but the wizard had moved to the edge of the ravine and was frowning down. "It seems to me there's a pattern to it," he said.

Cautiously, Pippin, Boldways and Kitty went to join him. There was dust in the air, and it was hard

to see … but Abacus was right. Each boulder swept
across from one bank to the other before swinging
round and thundering back again. What was
more – Pippin rubbed his eyes – it was
almost possible to believe the boulders
had faces; strange faces, with half-shut
eyes and twisted features … or was it
just his imagination?

"So…" Abacus cleared
his throat to get rid
of the dust.

"If we jump onto a rock as it turns, it should carry us across to the far side. It's just a question of timing!"

As Pippin peered down, the smell of frying bacon wafted towards him and made him whisk round. "Latterly?" he said, and ran to look. The little pot was full to the brim with bacon sandwiches.

Pippin's stomach rumbled in appreciation. "Bacon sandwiches are my absolute favourite," he said, and Latterly gave a small bounce in reply.

"Help yourself, Pippy Pip," she said, and winked at him. "Is nice for nicey niceness!"

Abacus, Kitty and Boldways had also been drawn towards the little iron pot. Abacus and Kitty ate their sandwiches with enthusiasm, but Boldways took a bite, then made a face.

"Yeuch! Mustard! Who made these? Far too much mustard!" And he threw the sandwich over the edge of the ravine.

The resounding CRASH! that followed made Pippin jump. There was a sudden surge of boulders, and now there was no doubt about it. They did have eyes and faces – and they also had huge open gaping mouths.

"What's happening?" Abacus clutched at Pippin's arm, his whiskers trembling and his hair standing on end.

Pippin didn't answer. A memory was stirring in his mind, and it took him a moment to work out what it was. Then it came to him. Chickens! One night he had forgotten to feed them, and when he had finally arrived with a bag of corn they had rushed at him in exactly the same desperate way. Still considering this idea, he picked up a second sandwich and hurled it as far as he could. The rocks hesitated … then swept away after it.

"Oi! What are you doing, boy?" Boldways was outraged. "I'm still hungry!"

"Look!" Pippin was alight with excitement. "The rocks are starving! If we feed them, they'll take us to the other side!" He turned to the little iron pot. "Latterly – dear Latterly – could you help?"

"You is my friend, Pippy Pip," Latterly said. "I helps my friends, I do."

"Could it be something I can throw?" Pippin asked. "Like … like doughnuts?"

Latterly's answer was to twirl round twice. This was followed by a mouth-watering smell of hot sugar, and a pot heaped high with jam doughnuts.

Abacus looked at Pippin with interest. "You've got a plan, haven't you, boy?"

"YES!" Pippin beamed. "Watch, Master." And he dropped a couple of doughnuts over the edge of the ravine.

The smallest boulders were the first to rush back, but they were quickly followed by the larger ones, and Pippin turned to the wizards and Kitty. "You see? If we jump on one of the big rocks we can get them to carry us across in exchange for doughnuts!"

Abacus clapped his hands.

"Excellent, my boy! Excellent!" And even Boldways gave a grunt of approval.

"Ready?" Pippin, Latterly in his arms, was poised on the edge of the ravine. "Look … that rock there! The one with the tufts of grass! It's big enough for all of us. Hey, Mr Rock! Would you like a doughnut of your very own?"

The rock edged even closer, and the two wizards, Kitty and Pippin stepped onto the rough grass that covered it.

"Mind my 'air," grumbled a voice from below. "'Ope you got clean feet. And give us another of them sugar buns!"

Pippin was so taken aback that he nearly dropped Latterly. "They can talk!"

Abacus nodded. "Better do as he asks, dear boy."

One by one Pippin dropped doughnuts in front of the rock, and slowly, weighed down by its passengers, it lurched across the ravine. From time to time its path was blocked by others hoping to share the treats, and Pippin was forced to toss extra doughnuts in their direction to distract them. He was growing increasingly worried about Latterly; her eyes were closed, and although the doughnuts kept coming they were getting smaller and smaller – and the rock was getting greedier and greedier.

They were only a little more than halfway across when she gave a little groan … and was empty.

"Give us some more!" rumbled the rock. "Give us some more!" And it stopped moving.

Boldways elbowed Pippin. "Do something!"

Pippin swallowed. It was obvious that Latterly was exhausted … but where could he get more food?

"OH!" A thought came to him and, hastily thrusting Latterly into Abacus' arms, he swung his bag off his back. The turnip pickle jar was still there; he pulled it out … then hesitated. It was very strong – might it have the wrong effect? There was only one way to know, and he twisted off the lid and poured the contents into the ravine.

The result was astonishing. There was a yell of disgust, and the rock took off at such a speed that Abacus and Boldways clutched each other for safety. Seconds later they were at the far side of the ravine, and Kitty had leapt onto the bank. As Pippin followed behind the two wizards, the rock twirled round and looked at him reproachfully.

A Very Special Turnip Pickle
A parting gift for Pippin

"You didn't 'ave to do that," it complained. "Me eyes is going to be watering for hours."

"I'm really sorry," Pippin apologized. "It was all I had left. It was my great aunt's turnip pickle."

"Packs a shocking punch," the rock said, and hiccuped. "Although…" a thoughtful expression crossed its stony face. "It don't 'alf clear the dust out of yer breathing tubes. Gor blimey! Do believe as I can smell the daisies! Got any more?"

"I'm afraid not," Pippin said. "But if ever I come this way again, I'll make sure I bring you another jar of it."

Kitty planted herself in front of Pippin. She had noticed the way Boldways had approved of Pippin's plan; Pippin had saved the day, and she hadn't … and she was angry with herself. What if Boldways decided to get rid of her? What would she do then?

"Hand over your invitation," she demanded. "We had a deal, remember?"

"What deal?" Pippin stared at her.

"If I got here first, I got the invitation," Kitty said.

Pippin shook his head. "I never said I agreed."

Kitty's eyes narrowed. "And you never said you didn't!"

Deciding it wasn't the right time to argue, Pippin pulled the invitation card out of his pocket. It was blank, and he began to move away from Kitty to see if the usual guiding letters appeared – but Kitty stayed close.

"Let me see!" she said, and snatched it out of his hand. "There's nothing on here! When you were reading it before, I could see letters that glowed – what have you done to it?"

"Nothing!" Pippin glared back at her. "And it's Master Abacus' invitation – so give it back!"

Kitty's temper flared, and she tore the card in half. One half she stuffed into her own pocket, the other she handed back to Pippin. "There," she said, with a triumphant smile. "Now you'll have to ask me every time you want to read it!"

Pippin swallowed hard. As Kitty bounded away, he stared miserably at the remains of the invitation.

"Boy!" It was Abacus. "Which way should we go, do you think?"

Pippin took a deep breath and guessed. "Erm … straight on, Master Abacus."

"Excellent!" Abacus nodded. "We're doing well – we can't be far away now."

"Yes, master," Pippin said. He looked round for Latterly, looked again – and gasped.

"Master! Where's Latterly?"

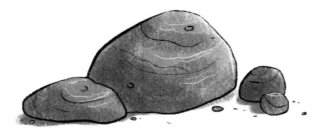

Chapter Thirteen

Pippin's heart was in his mouth as he looked at Abacus. "I gave her to you, Master – when I was looking for the pickle—" But Abacus' face was blank, and Pippin knew with a cold certainty that the wizard had forgotten.

He turned to look, and saw Latterly sweeping away on top of the rock they had travelled on. For a moment Pippin couldn't speak; he could only stare.

"Dearie me," Abacus said, and he shook his head. "A mistake to forget the pot, boy. Dearie me. What'll we do without her?"

Pippin's mind was whirling, but even as he tried to think what to do next, Kitty had seen an opportunity to impress Boldways Grime. Running down to the ravine, she leapt over the edge. Dancing lightly from one foothold to another she whirled and twirled her way to Latterly's rock, and then, clutching the little iron pot, she skipped her way back.

"There," she said, and she dropped Latterly at Pippin's feet. "Not so clever after all, are you?" She glanced at Boldways and saw, to her relief, that he was looking pleased.

Abacus stepped forward and clapped the elf on the back. "Well done," he said, "well done! Boy – you owe this young person a million thanks. Thank her, boy, thank her!"

"Thank you, Kitty. Thank you very much indeed." Pippin was squirming inside. He was hugely relieved to have Latterly safe beside him, but he was devastated that Abacus believed it was his fault that she had been left behind.

Boldways tut-tutted impatiently. "Now that my able assistant has rescued this pot of yours, Master Abacus, shall we continue on our way?"

"Yes, yes. Of course!" Abacus gave Pippin a sad smile. "Try not to mind too much, dear boy. I'm forgetful myself, you know. But do be careful."

After that, Abacus went silent – but Boldways Grime was whistling as he led the way up the slope and on to the narrow path at the top … a path that meandered in between thickets of gorse bushes covered in golden flowers.

"Master!" Kitty was balanced on a heap of stones. "I can see the wood! And it's tiny! Why's it called 'neverending' when it's so small?" She jumped down. "Why don't I run on ahead? I'll be out the other side in no time, and I can see what's there. All I can see at the moment is mist."

Boldways nodded. "Go."

Delighted, Kitty leapt away – and was out of sight in seconds.

Abacus looked after her admiringly. "Such a fleet-footed elf." His eye fell on Latterly. "Perhaps a meal might be possible? My stomach is rumbling like the rocks!"

Pippin shook his head. "She's worn out, Master Abacus."

"And whose fault is that?" Boldways snapped.

"What's done is done," Abacus said peaceably. "And the pot is still here."

Boldways snorted. "No thanks to that boy of yours! I'd have turned him into a slug for an hour or two to teach him a lesson."

Pippin swallowed. The disappointment in Abacus' eyes was making him feel terrible.

He looked down at Latterly and saw her wink at him before murmuring, "You crossed the rocky rocks, Pippy Pip. You crossed the rocks."

Pippin took a deep breath. Heartened, he tucked Latterly more firmly under his arm and set off after Master Abacus.

Chapter Fourteen

Kitty Scarper skipped merrily in between the trees, humming as she went. "I'm getting much better at being bad," she told herself. "I'm sure to be able to help Boldie win his competition, and then I'll get my reward … and after that I'll find another wizard to work for. Maybe a good one. But as long as I'm working for Boldie I'll be bad, bad, bad!"

Pleased with this decision, Kitty leapt onto a fallen tree and danced along the trunk. As she pirouetted off the end she was astonished to hear a voice.

"Help! Help!" The plea was followed by a series of plaintive squeaks, and Kitty peered into the tangle of roots, twigs and leaves. A bat was pinned down by a substantial root; when she saw Kitty she waved a hopeful wing. "Miss! Help me get out of here!"

"Yuck!" Kitty drew back in alarm. "You're covered in spots!"

For a moment she hesitated. Should she help the bat?

No, she told herself. *Someone bad would never do that*. In a moment the bat was forgotten. Thoughts of the future spurred her on, and she was humming again as she scampered between the tall trees.

Ten minutes later she found herself at the fallen tree trunk again. She rubbed her eyes – but there was no doubt about it. It was the same tree trunk. Could she have circled round?

"You're back!" The bat was delighted, but Kitty ignored her. Frowning, she looked to left, then right. That was the way she needed to go; she was certain of it. Shaking her head, she set off again.

The bat rubbed her aching stomach, and sighed. "She'll be back in two ticks," she told a passing beetle. "Just you wait and see."

It was longer than two ticks, but less than ten minutes before Kitty came bounding in between the trees. When she saw the tree trunk, she groaned.

"Hello," the bat said. "Going to help me this time? The name's Mavis, by the way. Who are you?"

Kitty didn't answer. She was inspecting a tall pine tree. "If I climb that, I'll be able to see the path! Why didn't I think of that before?"

She had spoken out loud, and Mavis snorted.

"This is the Neverending Wood, this is! Looks like nothing at all, but looks is deceiving, looks is. Need to be dead clever to get out once you're in."

"Well, I'm very clever," Kitty boasted, and she whisked her way to the top of the tree. Once there she looked round and, yet again, marvelled at how small the wood was. She could easily see the slope she had run down, as well as the mist hiding the view beyond. Why did she keep going wrong? Sliding down, she set off again.

Mavis sighed. It was getting dark, and her feet were aching badly. *If I don't get out of here soon*, she thought, *I'll be in real trouble.* She sighed again. *Me – Mavis Trueflitter – grounded, and all because I bit a wizard. If ever—*

Her thoughts were interrupted by the sound of flying feet … and a loud wail.

It was Kitty. The elf flung herself on the ground, and thumped it with her fists. "I can't find the way!" she yelled. "I'm going to be here for ever and ever and ever! It's a stupid, stupid, STUPID wood and I wish I'd never signed up to be a wizard's helper – if I ever get out of here I'm going home, home, HOME!"

"Wizard?" Mavis' ears pricked up. "You work for a wizard?"

Kitty lost her temper. "Be quiet! Horrible beastly thing – if I get spots and die it'll be all your fault!" And she began to cry hot angry tears.

By the time Abacus, Pippin and Latterly reached the edge of the wood, Boldways had found a small hollow, and settled himself in the most comfortable spot. He gave Pippin a cold stare.

"I don't know why you don't go home, boy. You're not wanted here."

Abacus raised a hand in protest. "The boy has been invaluable!" A cloud crossed his face.

"Although I can't quite bring to mind what he's been up to. Boy! Tell us! What have you done?"

Pippin blinked. "I helped you find the way, Master," he said, and put his hand in his pocket before remembering that the half card was useless.

It was too late. Abacus had visibly brightened, and was beaming at him. "Of course you did! Dear boy, tell us what lies beyond the wood. Have we much further to go?"

"Ummm…" Pippin got to his feet. "I'll … that is – I mean – I'll go away and read it. It works best if I'm on my own—"

Boldways had noticed his confusion, and sneered. "Is there a problem?"

Pippin gave Abacus an agonized glance, but the wizard didn't notice.

He put an arm round Pippin, and said, "I do believe you have a touch of magic in you, dear boy. Only those with true magic in their hearts can understand an invitation from the Head Wizard. Boy – give my fellow wizard the card."

He gave Boldways a low bow.

"Perhaps you would do us the honour of reading it?"

Boldways' jaw dropped, and there was the tiniest of pauses before he said smoothly, "No, no. The light is growing dim, and my eyes aren't what they were. Let the boy read it."

He cleared his throat while he tried to think of a way to change the subject.

"I would have expected Kitty Scarper to have returned by now," he said quickly. "Wherever can she be?"

Abacus looked blank. "Kitty? Kitty who?"

"My assistant." Boldways sounded irritated. "The elf."

"Oh yes, yes, yes." Abacus pulled at his beard. "And she's missing, you say? That's very worrying, very worrying indeed. We should go and search for her … we should go right now!"

Boldways shrugged. "Perhaps it was further than she thought."

Abacus stared at him. "But – dear sir! Alone, in the unknown darkness of the woods at night! There might be wolves … or bears." His old face creased in worry. "She could be in serious danger!"

His companion was unmoved. "I'm sure she can look after herself. Besides, she's only an elf."

And, ignoring Abacus horrified expression, he closed his eyes.

Chapter Fifteen

Unaware of her master's lack of concern, Kitty was curled up in a heap of leaves some distance from the fallen tree. She had decided not to make any further attempts to escape from the wood until morning. Mavis had tried to start a cheery conversation a couple of times, but Kitty had refused to answer, and the bat had all but given up.

"Thought you said you was working for a wizard," she remarked after a long silence. "Not got any magic skills yourself, then?"

There was no reply, and Mavis shrugged.

Folding her wings around her as best she could, she slipped into an uncomfortable doze.

At the edge of the wood Pippin, lying in the shadow of a tall tree, wasn't even trying to sleep. His head felt as if it was full of jagged pieces. If Kitty didn't come back soon the wizards were bound to ask him to find the way – and what could he say? If he explained that Kitty had torn the card in half not only would he be telling tales, but he was certain that Boldways wouldn't believe him. And suppose Kitty really was lost in the wood? He sat up, and stared into the darkness of the trees. What if he went to look for her?

As if in encouragement, the moon swung out from behind a cloud, and Pippin got to his feet. As he did so, a small voice murmured, "What doing, Pippy Pip?"

"I'm going to look for Kitty," Pippin said. "I can't sleep, and Master Abacus thinks she might be in danger."

"Don't get lost, Pippy Pip," Latterly told him. "Woods is tricksy, woods is. Lefty left seems righty right, and righty right is wrong, wrong, wrong."

Pippin thought for a moment, then picked up his shoulder bag. Fishing inside it he pulled out a ball of wool. "Look!" he said as he tied one end to the nearest tree. "I won't get lost now!"

"Goodly good." Latterly was approving, and Pippin smiled at her. Then, tiptoeing past the snoring wizards, he set off to look for Kitty.

It was darker in among the trees than he had expected, and for the first five minutes he was scratched by thorny bushes, and slapped at by low branches. He was beginning to wonder if he was ever going to make any progress, when the moon shone out once more, and the wood was washed in silver light. "Phew," he said, and quickened his step.

Was that a moan? Or some sort of night bird? Pippin froze, then tiptoed onwards, listening as he went.

There it was again! He stopped, and peered into the shadows. A fallen tree lay on the ground in front of him, and he was sure the sound had come from there.

"Hello?" Pippin was annoyed to find his voice was wobbling, and he tried again. "Hello?"

"Help!" The voice was a squeak. "I need some help!"

Pippin could see nothing. "Ermmm… Where are you?"

"Under a root. Over here!"

Pippin knelt down, and reached under the tree trunk. More by luck than judgement his hand found the small furry body and, very gently, he eased Mavis out. "Is that better?"

Mavis shook out her wings, and stretched her aching feet. "Ta ever so, Mister. Appreciate the help. Now, fair's fair. Are you lost, like the other one? Know these woods like the claws on my toes, I do."

Pippin was taken by surprise. "What other one?"

"Asleep over there. Thinks a lot of herself, she does. But –" Mavis sniggered – "she couldn't find her way to the other side of the wood, could she? Went round and round in circles, like they all do." With some difficulty, she fluttered onto Pippin's shoulder. "Ouch! Excuse me. Stomach's still playing up."

"Did you eat something bad?" Pippin asked, and the bat shook her head.

"Bit a wizard. Take my advice, and keep away from magic. Indigestible, magic is."

"Wizard? You bit a wizard?" In his surprise Pippin spoke more loudly than he had meant to, and Kitty stirred in the darkness … stirred, and sat up.

There was pride in Mavis' voice as she answered. "That I did. And not just any old wizard. It was the Head Wizard himself – and I'd do it again right now. Flicked me, he did, and I'm meant to be his pet! He did it once, and I told myself, just take it on the chin, Mavis old girl. But when he done it a second time – well. That was it. I bit him."

Pippin, his heart beating fast, sat down on the fallen tree. "So – you know the Head Wizard?"

"Nothing as I don't know."

The pride was back in Mavis' voice.

"Him and his cronies. Planning all sorts they were, last time I seed them."

"Did they…" Pippin was almost afraid to ask. "Did they mention a banquet?"

"Ho, yes! Never stopped!" Mavis made a rude noise. "Full of it, they were. Greedy pigs, all of them."

"And…" Once again Pippin hesitated. "Did they say where it was going to take place?"

"YES!" Kitty, quivering with excitement, arrived beside Pippin. "Where's the banquet?"

Mavis glared at the elf, and folded her wings over her chest. "Not telling."

"Tell me," Kitty said, "tell me now!" She lunged forward to grab the bat, but Pippin was too quick for her. He put up a protecting arm, and pushed her away.

"What's the matter with you, stupid boy?" Kitty asked angrily. "Don't you want to know?"

Pippin sighed. "Of course I do. But…" he paused. Did he dare tell her what he was really thinking? Taking a deep breath he said, "Have you ever thought of being nice to people … and bats? So they're nice back to you?"

There was a furious silence before Kitty said, "I'm going to find Master Boldways. He'll make that bat talk, and no mistake! Just you wait and see!" And she stamped away, muttering loudly as she went.

"She'll be back in the squeak of a bat's whisker, you wait and see." Mavis was chuckling. "The Neverending Wood, this is, so everybody walks in circles. Only a little wood, see, but it's dead clever when folks come blundering in. Round and round and round, they goes. Round and round and round."

"Really?" Pippin's eyes widened. "So are they here for ever?"

Mavis shrugged. "Every so often the wizards have a clear out, and send them home."

"If Kitty's really walking in circles I'm going to wait for her," Pippin said. "I can't leave her – that wouldn't be fair."

"If you have to." Mavis sounded disappointed. "Well, while we're waiting, what was it you wanted to ask me?"

Chapter Sixteen

Kitty had not gone far. She was angry with herself for losing her temper, and even more angry with Pippin for telling her off, as she had an uncomfortable feeling he was right. She had tried to kick her way through a thicket of briars, and the thorns had caught and held her until she had calmed down enough to wriggle out. As she did so she realized she could hear Pippin and Mavis talking, and she began to tiptoe back again.

"They'll be talking about the banquet…" She began to grin. "This is a much better way to find out what that bat knows!"

Closer and closer she crept, until she could hear clearly.

"They've put thick fog all round the outside wall of the wizards' centre," Mavis was explaining, "so the wizards don't know who's there." She giggled. "If you ask me, it's going to be a right laugh. Wizards all over the place, crashing about and bumping into each other – and nobody knowing who's number one hundred, and who's going to be turned into a tortoise."

Kitty silently punched the air. She had the information she needed; now all she had to do was get back to Boldways – but how could she avoid going round in circles again?

"That sounds dreadful." Pippin shook his head, then frowned. "Shouldn't Kitty be back by now?"

Mavis shrugged. "Give her another couple of minutes." She stretched her wings. "I'll get the two of you out – and then I'm off to see the family." She squinted over her shoulder. "Can't see properly. Would you say the spots are fading? Don't want to scare my poor old mum!"

"I can't see any spots," Pippin said. "And it's OK – I can find my own way out of here." He coughed modestly. "You see, I tied a strand of wool to my wrist. The other end's tied to a tree where Master Abacus is asleep."

"Clever boy," Mavis said. "There's not many as would think of a thing like that. Still, you be careful. I'll maybe pop back to check on you later." And with a wave of her wings she flittered up and away into the moonlit sky.

It was all Kitty could do not to whoop with excitement. She crept as near as she dared, and peered through the leaves.

The moonlight was bright, and she could just make out the strand of wool stretching away in between the trees. As silently as a shadow, she slipped from her hiding place, and followed the wool until there was no danger of being seen. Bending down, she picked up the thread and stared at it.

"Shall I leave it?" Kitty wondered – but then she remembered her resolution. "I'm bad!" she said. "That's what I am. I'm bad!" and before she could change her mind, she snapped the thread in two.

She had only gone a few steps when a terrible feeling of guilt swept over her. What if Pippin was never seen again? What if he was eaten by a bear? She stood very still, thinking. Then, with a sigh, she pulled the bag of peppermints out of her bag and dropped one on the ground ... and, as she reeled in the wool, she continued to drop peppermints behind her.

"There," she told herself as she came to the edge of the wood. "I've given him half a chance. I'm half good as well as half bad – so that's fair."

It was over half an hour before Pippin, cold and uncomfortable, decided there was no point in waiting any longer. With a sigh, he picked up the wool and began walking.

Suddenly, he found he was holding a frayed end. He searched among the fallen leaves for the other end, but it was pitch dark in the shadows, and he could see nothing.

"It must be here!" he told himself. Kneeling down, he felt frantically about – but he found no sign.

I'll have to wait until it's light, Pippin thought, and tried to ignore the thudding of his heart. *It's ever such a bright red... I'll be able to find it then. I... I don't suppose there are too many wild animals living here—*

A rustling noise made Pippin jump, and he swung round. As he did so a cloud covered the moon, and the shadows darkened ominously.

The rustling stopped, then started again.
Thoughts of wolves and bears floated into his
mind, and he trembled as he looked round for
a stick or a stone so he could defend himself.
It didn't sound like footsteps. It was more like
a heavy body dragging itself along—

"Pippy Pip?" The voice was wonderfully familiar,
and Pippin sank to the ground in relief.

"Latterly!" he said, and hugged her. "I'm SO
pleased to see you! Is Master Abacus here too?"

"No, Pippy Pip. I did come on my ownie own.
We is friends!"

Pippin sat down beside her. "We might be here
for a while. Everything's gone wrong."

The little iron pot made a sympathetic noise.
"Slippy slidey girl is bad, Pippy Pip."

"I know." Pippin hugged his knees. "She was
here in the wood, but I don't know where she is
now. Maybe she got to the other side, and we'll
meet her coming back."

Latterly sniffed. "No meety slidey girl. We hide."

That made Pippin laugh. "I'm so glad you're here. I was scared on my own."

He couldn't help but shiver.

"I kept hearing strange noises…"

There was a faint bubbling noise, and the suspicion of the smell of hot chocolate, but then it died away.

"I too tired, Pippy Pip," Latterly said apologetically. "I sorry."

"It's OK," Pippin told her. "Let's try and get to sleep. Hopefully it'll be morning soon…"

In the Centre for Wizarding Studies, Gloaming was pacing up and down trying to decide the best way to lead the wizards through to the gate.

"I'll put a green light over the arch," he decided. "A very bright green. They'll be able to see that, however thick the fog is."

Handily, dozing in his armchair, opened one eye. "Sounds all right. Have you set up my Tortoise-o-meter?"

"What?" Gloaming looked blank, and Handily sighed.

"The Tortoise-o-meter. I spent two days making it. It'll register the ninety ninth wizard as they get to this side of the gate. Makes a horrible noise – wails and moans and all that kind of thing – and then, ZAP! It changes the wizard into a tortoise."

"Oh, that." Gloaming nodded. "I've got it all set up. And I've got the prize-o-meter ready for the one hundredth wizard, same as always: there'll be loud cheers, peals of bells, trumpet fanfares, confetti all over the place. Strange… It was in perfect condition. You'd never think it hadn't been used for ninety-nine years."

Handily yawned again. "That's because the Head Wizard uses it to congratulate himself at least twice a week…" And his eyes closed.

Gloaming chuckled, and went to look for a bright green light.

Chapter Seventeen

As Kitty sped back through the trees she was trying hard not to worry about Pippin. Would he be all right?

"I don't care!" she told herself. "I'm bad! That's what I am … bad. And bad people leave other people to walk round and round a wood for ever, and they don't care! So there!"

When she reached the grassy hollow Abacus, wrapped up tightly in his wizard's coat, was fast asleep. Boldways, however, was sitting up and stretching. When he saw Kitty, he raised an eyebrow.

"Well? You took your time!"

Kitty put her finger to her lips. "I've got good news! We're nearly there, Master. The banquet's at the wizards' centre, on the other side of the wood. The Head Wizard's hidden it in a thick fog!"

Boldways stared at her. "Is this true?"

Kitty nodded. "I swear it is!"

Boldways Grime took a long deep breath, and his eyes gleamed as he thought of the room at the Golden Bean Hotel – a room he was going to sell for five hundred pieces of gold. Nothing, he told himself, was going to stand in his way now he was within reach of his goal. Nothing!

He leapt to his feet. "We must go! We'll hurry through the wood, and then we'll lurk … lurk and count the wizards as they arrive. Wake our companions!" He looked round. "But where's the boy?"

Kitty's smile widened. "Lost in the wood. Once you're there, you go round and round – that's why it's called the Neverending Wood.

Pippin thought he was SO clever:
he'd marked the way back with a bit
of wool! But I found it, and it showed
ME the way instead of him!"
Kitty waved the strand under
Boldways' nose, and
waited for him
to tell her how
well she had
done.

"I see." Boldways' voice was suddenly icy. "Have I heard you correctly? You left the boy in the wood?"

Kitty nodded. "He'll never find his way out now."

"I understand that." Boldways was looking grimmer than ever. "But how, exactly, are we going to reach the other side without him and his magic invitation?"

"Oh." Kitty shifted uneasily from foot to foot before an idea struck her. "But Master! Look!" She pulled the torn card from her pocket. "I've got one half, and he's got the other. He can't make it work without me; all we have to do is find him! And –" she thanked her lucky stars that she'd had a generous impulse – "I left a trail of peppermints, so we can find the way!"

"Hmmm…" Boldways considered for a moment. "Very well." He gave Kitty a look. "Just remember that the spell for turning elves into slugs is a remarkably easy one." His cackle of laughter made her shiver.

Abacus, shaken awake, looked round in surprise. "Is it morning?" he said. "But where is he? Where's my boy?"

"Pippin's waiting for us in the wood," Kitty told him, and he looked more confused than ever.

"In the wood? Then we must join him." As he began to get up, Boldways took his arm.

"Allow me," he said, and shook his head. "The journey has been long, Master Abacus. No wonder your mind wanders a little. But fear not! I will see you safely to the Wizards' Banquet." He turned to Kitty. "Now, lead us to the boy! And no dilly-dallying, or I'll make sure you grow horns and a shell…"

Chapter Eighteen

The first light of dawn was creeping into the wood when Pippin, after eating three very large bacon sandwiches, began to hunt for the missing strand of red wool.

He and Latterly were still searching for it when they heard the sound of voices, and looked up to see Boldways, Abacus and Kitty coming through the trees.

"Master Abacus!" Pippin said, and ran to meet him.

Abacus beamed with pleasure, and hugged him. "My boy!" he said.

Kitty, watching, bit her lip. She could never imagine Boldways Grime hugging her.

Boldways was also watching. "A delightful reunion," he said sourly. "But now we must hurry! We need to reach the wizards' centre before any other wizards arrive so we can count them in." With an effort he patted Pippin on the back. "Show us the path!"

Before Pippin could say anything, Kitty grabbed him by the arm and pulled him away from the two wizards. "Here," she said, and she pushed the other half of the invitation into his hand.

Pippin took it, and fitted the two halves together. As he did so, one edge flamed into gold, and he breathed a sigh of relief.

"This way," he said, and set off, Latterly trotting behind him. When they reached the fallen tree trunk where Mavis had been trapped, Pippin stopped. "This is where I found the bat who knew all about the wizards, Master."

"Might I rest a moment?" It was Abacus, and he sank down on the tree trunk with a weary sigh. "My old body is aching."

The little iron pot came trundling to his side. "Is hungry?" she asked, and when Abacus nodded she twirled round twice. "Cheesey weeze on toast!" she announced, and winked at Pippin as the wizards' faces lit up.

"Let me see!" Boldways leant over and helped himself. The next minute his eyes were streaming and he was gasping for breath. "Too much pepper! What's the matter with this pot? It's useless!"

Abacus, halfway through his second slice, stared. "But – dear friend! This is delicious!"

"Rubbish! It's disgusting!" Boldways glowered, and Abacus eyes opened wide.

"That's strange! Very strange. My little pot is trained to cook to a true wizard's taste." He held out a sandwich to Kitty. "Here, my dear."

"Ha ha!" Boldways wiped his eyes, and gave a hollow laugh. "Of course. I was joking. An excellent pot. Excellent indeed. So, shall we continue?"

Kitty, thoughtfully eating her toasted cheese sandwich, didn't answer, but Abacus pulled himself to his feet. "I'm ready."

With the magic invitation as a guide, it was only a short walk from the fallen tree to the edge of the Neverending Wood. Standing under the shade of a large oak, the travellers could see the fog in front of them; it was as if the Centre for Wizarding Studies was wrapped in thick white wool, and Abacus beamed. "We're here! Our journey is over!"

"Wow!" Pippin said. "How on earth are we going to find the gate?"

"There's a light, dear boy," Abacus told him, and he was right. There was a green glow in the distance; as they watched, it blinked three times, and then shone out again.

"That's the sign!" Abacus, his whiskers quivering with excitement, took Pippin's arm. "Stay close to me! And let's go—"

"Just one moment!" Boldways Grime stepped away from the rest of the party, and folded his arms. There was a triumphant gleam in his eyes as he snatched the invitation away, and said, "I fear, Master Abacus, that you're going to be disappointed. I should thank you and your boy for leading me here. However, being of sound mind and body, I can count to one hundred – so now I have no use for any of you. No use at all." He waved his arm, and—

WHOOOOOOOOOSH… BANG!

Chapter Nineteen

The purple, red and green sparkles gradually faded, and Pippin rubbed his eyes and sat up. Where was he?

"That was a bit speedy. In a hurry, was you?" Mavis was perched on the end of the fallen tree.

"What happened?" Pippin rubbed his eyes again. "How did I get here?"

"Magic, I'd say." Mavis put her head on one side. "I was just popping down to check as you was safely out of here, and you was, and then – wham bang! Cloud of sparks, and you was all of a heap on the ground! Just like the other ones!"

"Other ones?" Pippin was still dizzy.

"Her what was here before. The one who went round and round and round." Mavis pointed a wing, and Pippin saw Kitty propped up against a tree, her eyes shut. "And there's the little old whiskery one." Mavis pointed in the other direction, and Pippin gasped. Master Abacus was flat on his back, only the trembling of his whiskers showing that he was alive.

"Both still under the spell, I'd guess." Mavis nodded wisely. "Takes it out of you. The Head Wizard, was it? Up to his old tricks again? Thought he'd be too busy, what with his banquet and all."

"It was Boldways Grime," Pippin said. "He's trying to win the prize, but I'm going to stop him if it's the last thing I do."

"Mess with magic, and it most likely will be," Mavis said cheerfully. "Look! That one's beginning to wake up!"

Mavis was right. With a groan, Kitty opened her eyes and stared round.

"Are you all right?" Pippin asked.

Kitty shook her head. "I'm… I feel weird. Where are we?"

"In the Neverending Wood," Pippin told her, and Kitty groaned again.

"Then we'll be here for ever and ever." She tried to get up, but her legs were too wobbly and she sat down again. "Who were you talking to?"

"Mavis," Pippin said. "The bat."

"The one as you didn't want to help out of a little difficulty." Mavis gave Kitty a meaningful look. "And what I says is, what goes around comes around."

Kitty's head was spinning. "I don't know what that means."

"She means," Pippin said, "that you didn't help her, and now you're in trouble – so she won't help you."

"Nicely put." Mavis waved a wing. "Of course, having been brought up proper I'm always willing to give folks the benefit of the doubt – if an apology is offered, that is."

There was a silence. Pippin looked hopefully at Kitty; Mavis cleaned her claws.

Kitty put her hand to her aching head. "Boldways Grime never meant to give me any kind of reward, did he? He was just using me."

"Using all of you." Mavis was blunt. "Can't think how he got invited to the banquet. That's a bad wizard, if ever I saw one."

Kitty looked at her feet. "He wasn't invited. He's trying to trick his way in."

"Oh!" Pippin stared at her. "So why were you working for him?"

Kitty shook her head. "It was a job. I thought it would be fun being bad." She swallowed. "But it wasn't."

"Ahem." Mavis had been listening with interest. "Do I spot a teensy change of heart? Are we sorry that we was nasty to a small defenceless bat?"

There was a pause, then Kitty said grudgingly, "Yes. All right then. I'm sorry. I suppose I could have—" She was interrupted by a loud groan, and Abacus sat up.

"Where am I?" He looked wildly round. "Where's this?"

"We're back in the Neverending Wood," Pippin told him. "Master Boldways magicked us here."

Abacus stared at him. "He did?"

Kitty made a face. "He's bad. He wants the prize for himself."

"Oh dear, oh dear, oh dear." Abacus heaved a huge sigh. "Oh dearie, dearie me. I was so hoping to win that room at the Golden Bean Hotel."

"No!" Pippin jumped to his feet. "We're going to get there, Master Abacus, and you're going to win!" He bent down, and looked at Latterly. She was covered in dust, and had her eyes shut.

"Dear Latterly! Are you all right?"

"I is still twirly whirly," she said. "Twirly whirly all over."

"I'll carry you," Pippin told her. He turned to Mavis. "We'd be ever so grateful if you could show us the way."

The bat looked pleased. "Favours done is favours owed," she told him. "Be my pleasure. Want to get back to the centre, do you?"

"Yes please," Pippin said, and Kitty, after a moment's hesitation, put her arm through his.

"We're ready!"

"So! Got yourself a team!" Mavis flew up into the air. "This way, me ducks!"

Chapter Twenty

It wasn't long before Mavis had led the team to
the edge of the wood, and once again they stared
into the dense white fog. The green light was still
signalling, and although nothing could be seen
there was now the sound of muffled footsteps
and voices.

"Sparkling spillikins! Can't see my hand in front
of my face! Is that you, Wuzzlegrim?"

"Excuse ME! That was my foot!"

"Head for the green light! Head for the green—
OW! Watch where you're going!"

Kitty looked at Pippin. "So what do we do now?"

Pippin rubbed his ear. "I don't know…"

"Tsk, tsk." Mavis was disapproving. "Buck up! Think of something!"

"Umm…" Pippin rubbed his ear again, then brightened. "Mavis! Could you fly over the fog? Can you tell us what you can see?"

"That's better." Mavis nodded. "Here goes!" And she was off, flying high. Moments later she was back. "Easy peasy! That fog – it's no higher than the top of a wizard's pointy hat!" She gave Abacus a dismissive glance. "Not like his. But the tall ones."

"Really?" Pippin's mind began to whirr. "Would Kitty be able to see if I lifted her up?"

Kitty seized his arm. "Only one way to find out!"

"Be careful, my dear!" Abacus warned as he took Latterly out of Pippin's arms, but Kitty took no notice. The next minute she was standing on Pippin's shoulders, looking round.

"The bat's right!" She began to giggle. "It's a sea of starry hats … although I can only see the pointed tops."

"Can you count them?" Pippin asked.

"Yes… No." Kitty sounded disappointed. "They're already going through the arch."

Pippin considered. "What if we get really near the gate, so that we can see when Boldways is getting ready to go through? Would you recognize Boldways' hat?"

Kitty snorted. "I should do. I've had to clean it often enough."

Mavis flew down and settled on Kitty's shoulder. "Oooh! Bat's eye view, you've got now, ducky."

Abacus was looking anxious. "We must stay close together, my dears. If we get separated we'll never find each other again."

"Be very, very careful, Pippy Pip!" Latterly was worried too.

"Hang on a minute … the hats are thinning out now," Kitty reported. "The ones left must be the ones who want to win the prize. They dither about, then make a dash to go through. OH!" She lowered her voice. "I can see Boldways' hat! He's right by the gate – all set to be the one hundredth wizard!"

"Oh. Oh … oh… OH!" Pippin was so excited that he was shaking, and Kitty fell off his shoulders with a squeal of indignation.

"Oi! What did you do that for?"

"I've had an idea!" Pippin was glowing. "He's waiting for the ninety-ninth wizard, isn't he? Well –

suppose WE'RE the ninety-ninth? Boldways will come in after us, thinking he's won – but Master Abacus will wait behind him – and HE'LL be the real winner!"

Kitty stared at him. "Are you mad? And what do you mean, WE?"

"You get on my shoulders again, and we'll wear Master Abacus' coat – it's meant for someone much taller than him – and his hat!"

Kitty frowned. "And get turned into a tortoise."

"I don't think we will." Pippin crossed his fingers, hoping he was right. "We're not wizards. As soon as we're on the other side, and Boldways has come through the gate, we'll show ourselves for what we are!"

"Hmmmm." Kitty still looked doubtful, and Pippin turned to Abacus.

"They wouldn't turn us into tortoises, would they, Master Abacus?"

Abacus pulled at his beard. "I doubt it, dear boy, but I really can't promise…"

"It don't last for ever," Mavis put in. "Being a tortoise, that is. Magic wears off after a few weeks—"

"WEEKS?" Kitty went pale.

"Oh… PLEASE!" Pippin begged. "It'll be fine – I know it will!"

There was a very long pause, then Kitty said, "All right. But if I do get turned into a tortoise I'll… I'll BITE you!"

"It's a deal," Pippin said. "And now – Master Abacus – could we borrow your coat and hat?"

Chapter Twenty-One

Boldways Grime was not comfortable. He had been standing as close to the gate as he dared, ever since the first wizard blundered his way through: his eyes were watering and his nose running, but he was too terrified of losing count to do anything about it.

Once he had sniffed, and a sharp voice had asked, "Who's that? Don't dilly-dally! Come through the gate!" Fortunately for Boldways a large and hairy wizard had chosen that moment to stomp past, loudly claiming the prize, and he had remained undiscovered.

"Ninety-three, ninety-four," he counted as the gate opened and closed. "Ninety-five. Ninety-six, ninety-seven…" A quiver of excitement ran up his spine. "Not long now…"

A small wizard was dithering. Boldways heard him muttering to himself: "I think I'm the one hundredth! I really think I am! But am I right? There doesn't seem to be anyone behind me… I'm almost sure there's nobody behind me…"

Boldways smiled a sour smile.

"So – should I risk it?" the wizard went on. "Should I? Oh! I don't know if I should or not!"

Suppressing a strong desire to push the hesitant wizard through the gate by force, Boldways held his breath.

"I will! I will!" And then there was the reassuring sound of the gate being opened, and the *clang!* as it closed.

"Ninety-eight." Boldways allowed himself a sigh of relief, and waited. Who would be the ninety-ninth? Who was going to be turned into a tortoise, and excluded from the wonders of the feast?

*   *   *

Pippin, Kitty on his
shoulders dressed
in Master Abacus'
coat and hat, was
only just able to see
where he was going.
As they approached
the gate his knees
began to tremble,
and for a dreadful
moment he thought
he might collapse
before they got
through. It was
lucky Kitty was so
light; his shoulders
ached, but it was
bearable … for the
moment.

"Bend your knees!"
Kitty hissed at him.

"Bend your knees! There's an arch, and I don't want my head knocked off!"

Pippin did as he was told, and a moment later felt the cold metal of the gate under his hand. Fumbling, he found the latch and, heart thumping wildly, clicked it open.

"Here we go," he muttered.

Boldways, surrounded by mist, held his breath. Had he heard footsteps? He strained his ears. Yes! And the gate was creaking open. YES! Now the gate was closing – he could hear the clang as it closed behind the ninety-ninth wizard.

With a triumphant shout, he strode towards the arch and through the gate, puffing out his chest, swirling his cloak, and waiting for the sound of celebratory bells and trumpets…

But instead there was an ear-splitting wail, followed by howling noises.

Boldways felt himself shrinking, down, down, down … and when he looked at his hands they were small and leathery, and there was a heavy weight on his back…

With his last breath as a wizard he whispered, "Tricked! I've been tricked!" And then he was a tortoise, and a large green goblin was carrying him away to eat lettuce.

A minute later there was the sound of wild cheering as the celebratory bells began to ring, the trumpets blew, multi-coloured confetti filled the air … and Pippin and Kitty heard a familiar voice asking, "Are you all right, my dears?"

Chapter Twenty-Two

Pippin and Kitty stared in amazement as they walked into the Centre for Wizarding Studies behind Abacus.

The banquet was a wonderful sight. The table stretched from one end of the Great Hall to the other, and was laden with every kind of delicacy that could be imagined. Puddings and pies of every kind were piled high, and there were vats and vats of spicy steaming stew. Plates groaned under the weight of sizzling sausages, cauldrons bubbled, and multi-coloured jellies wobbled on silver platters. There were cakes glittering with sugar, crispy biscuits fresh out of the oven, bowls and bowls of glossy chocolate mousse, jugs of thick yellow cream, and a towering ice sculpture in the shape of Philostrate Bodiface.

"Got a drip on the end of its nose," Mavis remarked. She was still on Kitty's shoulder, and was enjoying herself immensely. "Typical."

Pippin had never seen such a vast display of food, and his stomach rumbled loudly. Latterly, at his feet, chuckled. "Goodly good good goodest, Pippy Pip. Is where I come from! I see friendy friends! Is time to be go go going!" And before Pippin could ask what she meant, she had trundled away.

Abacus, who was now wearing an enormous gold medal announcing that he was the one hundredth wizard, looked after her in astonishment. "Well I never! Was that a goodbye?"

Pippin blinked. "I hope not. I'm very fond of her."

Abacus nodded. "Me too, dear boy. But now I do believe the Head Wizard is going to speak."

Abacus was right. The Head Wizard was standing at the head of the table, and he surveyed his guests with a superior smile.

"Welcome, one and all! And a special welcome to Master Abacus Peridot, a worthy winner of the room at the Golden Bean Hotel."

There was loud applause, and Abacus blushed, and pulled at his beard.

"I also," Philostrate went on, "wish to welcome two unexpected visitors, Kitty Scarper, and

Pippin Potts. It is entirely due to the ingenuity of these young people that an imposter wizard has been caught – caught, and suitably punished. A few weeks as a tortoise will, without a doubt, encourage him to mend his ways."

There was a burst of applause, and the Head Wizard looked pleased. "Thank you. But let us return to Pippin and Kitty … because I would like to offer them both a permanent place here at the centre, to learn wizarding skills of every variety."

Pippin gasped. "WOW! Thank you. Thank you so much!"

But Kitty hesitated. "Thank you," she said. "I'd like to say yes, but I should probably tell you that I'm half bad." She twisted her fingers. "I was… I was turned down by the Fairy Godmothers' Guild."

To her astonishment the Head Wizard began to laugh – laugh so loudly that he began to hiccup, and had to be banged on the back by Gloaming.

"That, my dear young person, is the perfect qualification. I myself am half bad. What we must always remember is that we are also half good!"

"Oh." Kitty beamed at him. "Then yes please. I'd love to study here!"

"Then that's agreed. And now –" Philostrate clapped his hands – "I declare the Wizards' Banquet open!"

The banquet was a huge success. Even the Head Wizard's closing speech, lasting over an hour, couldn't spoil Pippin and Kitty's happiness. Abacus had invited Pippin to visit any time he wished, and Pippin had promised to come at least once a week.

"And you, my dear?" Abacus asked Kitty as the Head Wizard finally sat down. "You, too."

"Ummmm…." Kitty shifted uncomfortably. "Are you sure you'd want me to visit? I rather thought you might be cross with me…"

Abacus shook his head. "We all make mistakes. Without you and Pippin, I'd never have won the prize. And, of course –" he smiled at Mavis – "this excellent bat."

Mavis, perched on the back of Kitty's chair, nodded. "Never a truer word was spoke." She gave Kitty an approving look. "We all got good bits and bad bits. Even me. But now that's settled, I'll be off home … but I'll be popping by, regular like. See how you're doing." And with a flutter of wings, she flew up and away.

There was a meaningful cough from somewhere near Pippin's feet, and he looked down. "Latterly! I thought you'd gone!"

"Gone, Pippy Pip? Where to? I is chat chat chatting, is all. I is always here for you, Pippy Pip. And –" Latterly paused – "for Kitty Kit too. Her not slippy slidey now."

"Really?" Pippin was delighted. "That's wonderful." He looked round, smiling his widest smile. "You know what? This is the best day of my life. The very best."

Abacus chuckled. "Nonsense, dear boy. It's not the best day. It's your first day – your first day of living happily ever after."

"Hippy happy Pippy Pip and Kitty Kit," Latterly agreed. "And hippy happies need cake." At once there was a delicious smell of fresh baking – and there, in front of Pippin and Kitty and Abacus, was the most wonderful cake they had ever seen.

Iced on the top, in loopy writing, there was a message…

Vivian French

lives in Edinburgh and writes in a messy workroom stuffed full of fairy tales and folk tales – the stories she loves best. She's brilliant at retelling classic tales, as she did for *The Most Wonderful Thing in the World*, and has created worlds of her own in *The Adventures of Alfie Onion, The Cherry Pie Princess, Tom & Tallulah and the Witches' Feast* and *The Giants' Tea Party*. Vivian teaches at Edinburgh College of Art and can be seen at festivals all over the country. She is one of the most borrowed children's authors in UK libraries, and in 2016 was awarded the MBE for services to literature, literacy, illustration and the arts.

Marta Kissi

is a wonderfully talented illustrator, who came to Britain from Warsaw to study Illustration and Animation at Kingston University, then took an MA in Visual Communication at the Royal College of Art. *The Wizard's Banquet* is her sixth book with Vivian French; her other work for children includes books by Sophie Kinsella, Gillian Cross, Marcus Rashford and Olympian Mo Farah. She shares a studio in Bath with her husband and their pet plant, Trevor.